Welcome to the world of The Automatons

This book is the third of the Automatons series and takes place after both Haven House and Nobel Crest.

While the book *can* be read on its own, there are concepts and people in the Haven House and Nobel Crest which build the world of where men control every decision.

The Automatons Series

It takes strong women to bring down a world ruled by cults

Haven House

In a world where anything is possible, sometimes the worst comes at the hands that should care for you the best.

When Amaryllis Coultihan fled Haven House after Travis Haven threatens to make her one of his many brides, it straight into the arms of Gloriana, the woman who had married her brother, Andrew. Although her brother and sister-in-law insist she's safe, Ammy would rather die than allow herself to be swallowed by the evil of Haven House.

Damien Whitmore is a ranger, working undercover to bring down the religious cults, like Haven House and save the women trapped in them from a life of degradation. He's there when Amaryllis Coultihan escapes. While she may no longer be in Haven House, the malevolence that lurks within follows them, threatening her and the 5 children she fosters—also escapees of the Haven cult.

They might run, he might even shelter them, but while Amaryllis and Damien's feelings grow and blossom, so does the danger chasing them.

Nobel Crest

Evil across generations is an ugly thing, but even more so when rational thought it absent.

The adopted daughter of Amaryllis and Damien Whitmore, Francesca has a lot to prove, not only to herself and the world, but also to the Nobel family. When Adam, the patriarch of Nobel Crest took her under his wing, the whispers started, and they didn't end at his death. Now as a trained Physiotraducere, she's making a difference in people's lives... not just by aiding them after the loss of a limb, but also running the Whitmore Foundation.

Raphael Nobel thought the worst of Francesca. He bought into the idea that she'd used his father, and after the reading of the will, allowed himself to be used by his brother, Edward, now head of the house. Meeting her years later, he realises the mistakes he's made. When Damien asks him to protect Francesca from Travis Haven—a man with a grudge against the Whitmore family, he accepts.

Now, with the safety of Francesca, danger on every front and his brother's interference, they need help, because there's so much more than Nobel Crest at stake. The survival of their hearts are too.

Warning: This book contains cultist and coercive scenes some may find distressing.

Casa Bonita

In a world ruled by men, it takes strong women and the men who fight beside them to correct the injustices of the cult.

Constance returns to her family from London with a treasure that might just save them all. Like all the woman who sought shelter away from Haven House, she is broken. Damaged by her experiences, and she knows that love and marriage will never be on her horizon. Content to be the spinster art, she hones her craft with a needle.

Matteo is a second son, one who broke away from Casa Bonita, but he's not without plans. He wants to free those who remain on the island, to give others a future... Content to wait for a future where he might one day meet a woman who if not completes him, will give him a family. That is until he meets Constance, the intriguing daughter of Damien and Amaryllis Whitmore.

But taking down one of the most heavily fortified enclaves will require something special, the item only Constance can provide. But the road to safety—and love—is paved with danger.

Casa Bonita

by

Imogene Nix

Ebook: 978-1-922369-69-7

Paperback: 978-1-922369-70-3

Editing by Pamela Tyler

Cover by Dexpress Covers

Artificial Intelligence Statement

Imogene Nix does not use any form of AI in the production of her titles, nor is any form used in the production of her cover art and any associated aspect of production or marketing.

Imogene uses ethical procurement processes for the procurement of stock images for the production of cover art. No warranties or guarantees can be made for image creation beyond Imogene's control.

Please note:

The UK and USA share the English language, but there are many words that are spelled differently. Some words have extra letters in the British spelling, such as the word cancelled. In American English, it is spelled canceled. There are also words that interchange the letters c or s and sometimes z. For example, in America, you spell offense and in Britain, it is written as offence.

Examples of words you'll see in the book include: kerb, litre, centre, manoeuver, travelling and colour.

These spellings are **not** incorrect.

This book is written in UK English to reflect my Australian/English background.

Thank you to my family for your unwavering support. I could never achieve what I have without you on my team.

Thank you also to my Makers & Fakers tribe. You encourage me daily, you make me smile and that means the world to me.

To my readers, thank you for taking a chance on my books. You get me up in the morning and keep me gainfully occupied!

Imogene Nix
Taabinga 2024

BioCybe
Imo
A Merry
low
VEL
NIX
RE
R - BOOK 2
HAVEN HOUSE
IMOGENE NIX
WITH BONUS NOVELLA
STAR OF THE FLEET
IMOGENE NIX
Sexy Sassy Romance is only a click away!
Newsletter Sign Up
https://imogenenix.net/newsletter-2/

Chapter One

SITTING IN THE SMALL PARLOUR, waiting for Aunt Gloriana, wasn't quite what Constance had in mind when she returned from her sojourn in London, so this chafed. Badly. Three and a half years studying the art of clothing manufactory and she'd returned to be... the good daughter? *Nope.* Constance was up and heading for the door when the sound of footsteps had her turning. *Why break with a tried-and-true tradition now?* Constance stifled a snort.

Her father, Damien, entered the room. "Connie, my love!" He moved quickly, tugging her into a fierce hug, and she welcomed it. It had been far too long since anyone had held her so carefully.

"So, Papa, I'm back." She smiled and waited for his response.

"I thought it was only meant to be a year?" He quirked a brow, but it was softened by a wry smile.

"Well, the reality was, there was more to learn, and still more to try. Besides, you gave permission for me to extend it..."

He nodded. "Indeed, I did, but I missed you, Con." He released her, and she noted that his dark hair was now threaded with silver. "The others will be here soon. Oh, and Frannie and Raphael sent their apologies. It will be the weekend before they can get away. Her workload has increased, and Raphael is busy with Nobel Crest."

Francesca was her older half-sister, born to their mother by her first husband. When he'd died, their mother had been 'gifted' by the Master of Haven House to a new husband—her father and the father of her siblings. They'd been adopted by Ammy—Amaryllis—and Damien, then their life changed substantially.

"Constance?" Damien's words pulled her from the memories of near destitution.

"Sorry, wool-gathering. I brought presents—"

Damien smiled. "I know. The men are bringing the chests up in the morning, and your trunks... *There's four of them!*"

She trilled laughter at the horror in his words. "I said there were gifts. Plus, I had a set of the latest fitting equipment, machine sewers, and dress forms included. Oh, and some specialist materials which I think will surprise even you."

When he stared at her, and responded, "I hardly think materials will set my heart rate beating faster," she giggled.

"This material just might." Constance grinned.

More footsteps echoed and voices too. The thump she associated with Ammy, some lighter steps too.

"And they descend," Damien said as he swung open the door.

Ammy entered, a vision in pale blue chiffon and lace. "Dearest Connie! You're home."

Constance found herself enveloped as one by one members of the family greeted her, including Dawn, who'd grown so much since she'd left, and Aunt Gloriana.

"Mama says you're not going anywhere ever again," Dawn said, and Constance raised a brow and glanced at Amaryllis.

"We'll see, but for now, here I am, and I have presents." Constance looked to the staff gathered by the door. "For everyone. Millie, if you'd open the green trunk, and disperse the gifts, and Fred and James, would you mind bringing the red and white striped chests in?"

The chests were duly carried in, and she heard the staff cooing and gasping as their items were inspected, while the two men carried in the other trunks she requested, then they withdrew from the room, closing the door behind them.

"I thought long and hard about what to bring back. Faith, you're first," Constance said, opening the lid of the red trunk. "Gowns from Paris and London. Only a few, but I can make more." The parcel wrapped in brown paper and tied with a bright red ribbon was passed over. "I also found smocks for you, to cover your gowns."

"Oh, thanks, Con. Me and dresses, they tend to get a little singed," Faith answered as she unwrapped the package. "Oh, the patterns. So intricate." Her fingers traced the velvet.

"Ammy, for you. Tea gown, ball gown, and of course a visiting ensemble in your favourite colours. Aunt Gloriana, I've a ball gown and visiting gown for you too." Once more, packages emerged, tied with floral bows. For Dawn there was new boots, a riding habit, and day dresses. Francesca's bundle remained in the trunk. "I'll give it to her when she arrives," Constance said, and she pushed aside two more smaller bundles. "Now, Father, for you and the boys, I have something very special."

Damien's brow quirked. "Special, is it?"

She nodded, belly knotting until she was sure they understood its importance and passed them each their own packages.

Damien opened his. "It's a coat and trousers?" He seemed perplexed.

"In London I came across a man selling this cloth. It's ballista graded..." She waited for realisation to dawn.

"Ballista?" Damien clarified.

"Yes."

Ammy screwed up her nose. "What is ballista?"

Damien smiled. "It means that we'd be protected from things that might penetrate the body. You're making us weapon-proof." He advanced and took Constance's hand.

"Not quite, but it will make you impervious to most of the hand-held weaponry on the areas covered by the fabric. I'm also working on a design for facial coverings." She shrugged. "I brought extra material back, so I can make more, and I have details of a supplier for mass production at a later point. He's willing to work with me as the only importer of this product, for a fee."

Damien's eyes gleaned. "Ah, business to discuss. We can talk about this later, but yes, I'm very much interested."

Matteo snorted as he considered the documents delivered to him. "You're sure these figures are right? I don't want to be—"

"I wouldn't be giving them to you if they weren't. Our people are in positions to have the facts, not to guess, Matteo. The men aren't ready yet to take on the battle. It's too soon after the deaths of the women."

Closing his eyes, Matteo counted to fifteen. Ten wasn't enough to wash off the fury that still coursed his veins. Haven House and Nobel Crest had both been wins for those who wanted to destroy the system of power the men of the SELED—also known as the 'Sect Leader Delegates'. Each house had its own hierarchical system of power, and the apex was the master. Matteo had left Casa Bonita years ago, but was determined to ensure that he could join the powers fighting to dismantle the system Casa Bonita had been created under.

Three years ago, Casa Bonita had taken Edward Nobel in. He'd been furious and deeply unsettled. Then he'd begun killing, slaughtering women until he'd been stopped, death having been the final solution.

The fallout within Casa Bonita had led to a power shift, and destabilisation.

"Casa Bonita isn't the house it once was. It's weak." Matteo tapped a finger on the desk. "It's ripe, but we can't just storm in and take control, unless we are totally sure we'd successfully overthrow the existing power base. Our work must be quiet, and cautious. Once we are confident—"

"But time is of the essence. We know there's something brewing, and the strides we've taken to free those caught up against their will... the plan will be endangered." Once more the man cleared his throat. "I know you've an idea, but..." He shrugged.

"None of these plans can be made in haste, Ellis. You know that," Matteo said.

Ellis grunted and settled himself in the seat opposite with a hiss.

"Your injury still pains you." Matteo's statement was joined with a frown.

"Frannie said it likely always will. The injuries... She told me afterward that I was lucky to survive." Ellis shrugged his shoulders and stared at Matteo.

"She's the best physiotraducere in our system. Bloom has sent her and Raphael into many situations...."

"Not anymore. She's expecting and Raphael is hovering."

Matteo didn't miss the smile on the other man's face. He knew of the amazing work Francesca Whitmore-Nobel did with those injured in the clashes between Bloom's men and the SELED. It didn't really surprise Matteo though, because the work of Damien and Amaryllis Whitmore in the deregistration of certain SELED houses had broken new ground. Damien's manufacturing of weaponry designed to assist in the not-so-infrequent skirmishes was integral to their purpose.

"So, we have an agreement. You'll apprise Bloom of my plans?" Matteo pushed the younger man.

"I will, but I believe it's his hope that somehow this will be brought to a head sooner rather than later." Ellis rose. "I'm off then. Raphael has arranged a speedy dirigible for me, as I have another side task to achieve before I report to Bloom."

Matteo frowned. "You found her?"

Ellis shook his head. "No. Not yet, but I will. Then I'll make sure she has everything she needs."

Matteo bit back a response. Ellis' personal mission? To find the young girl he'd been sweet on before his injury. Her abduction had spiked the final push to free Nobel Crest. Edward Nobel had flown to Casa Bonita, and Matteo's father, Inigo, had welcomed the man into his own flock. The same way he had welcomed others with dark and brutish intentions.

Ellis retreated and Matteo sat at the desk, considering what he'd learned and what must be his next steps in his mission from Bloom.

Free Casa Bonita.

Three words. Easy to say but so much harder to achieve. Haven House had been a bloodbath; Nobel Crest had been released with a whimper. But the holdings Inigo kept out of sight would make Casa Bonita near impossible to achieve. Unless something gave.

Matteo needed to talk to Damien Whitmore.

Chapter Two

HER RETURN to the place she called home felt anti-climactic to Constance. The flight by dirigible had taken days, where she'd paced and packed and considered how to explain to Damien what she felt so strongly about. Her place in the family was... what? A grown daughter with no real ambition? Except making clothes. "I'm more than that," she scoffed, but it didn't change the fact that her early childhood had scarred her. Toughened her. Given her a purpose that not everyone could or would understand.

She remembered the days before Ammy and Damien so well. She didn't talk about them, but the knowledge sat deep in her psyche. She'd seen the decline of her birth mother, the squalor they'd existed in.

Then Damien and Ammy had come along, adopted her and her siblings, but even that hadn't been straightforward. After they'd been saved, her life had changed, become a world where little wasn't achievable. A world of comfort, food, and education. Opportunities. "But I don't forget," she whispered into the wind.

London had been different. "And I didn't expect that, not at all." The old world hid a sub-culture of scientists and inventors, always looking for something new to test or try or invent. Something to change the world. Before she'd made the trip, she'd never considered herself anything out of the ordinary, her mettle existed below the surface but had never had to show itself.

Not until she'd met Lillian, Sacha, and Laura. They'd opened her eyes to a world where nothing was out of reach to the average person. Once again, the benefits of Ammy and Damien as parents opened doors for her.

Constance hovered near the doorway of the salon, her guard, Anderton, in the background. Ever watchful, he was the shield at her back, even when she didn't need one. The room was luscious with plush carpets, deep red walls, and the sconces on the walls lit by a new iridescent light, and they appeared to twinkle.

"Come, Constance. Raphael sent word that you should receive entrée into society. That means you need to come away from the doorway." Lady Sacha Cartwright giggled. "Besides, that gown you designed is so fetching. You simply must parade so others may see your fine work."

Her hand was grabbed by Sacha who dragged her into the middle of the room. "But Sacha…"

"Nonsense. Now come, meet my friends, Laura and Lillian. I told you about them when you arrived, and I've allowed you a week to catch your breath, refurbish your wardrobe, and to rest. Now you simply must mingle after you meet them." Sacha linked their arms together, and Connie wondered how this woman, Raphael's cousin, could possibly have married a Lord when she positively had too much sass.

"Come now, here's Lillian! Sweet girl, here she is. My friend Constance."

"Oh my, Sacha. She's so pretty, but that gown? It's positively breathtaking. Where did you—"

"She made it, Lilli. I mean, how amazing is this gown?" Sacha giggled. "It's simply divine, but the pieces she's crafting for me? It'll make the rest of society positively green with envy!"

Constance shifted on the spot as her face flamed.

"Truly? Oh, my word, it's exquisite," Lillian trilled.

"I was planning to introduce her to Laura."

Lillian grinned. "You're thinking the material her father assisted her with?"

Sacha nodded. "Exactly. Imagine if we have someone with the skills and ability to create the clothing we discussed."

Meeting Sacha, Lillian, and Laura had changed Constance's view of the world. Laura had created a material with input from her father, who was the exporter she was dealing with. The material was found to be impervious to handheld armaments. It took years to work out the best way to cut and sew the material. Among the issues was ensuring seams were strong enough to withstand the shock of impact while its weight made it uncomfortable to wear when used for standard designs. Constance had made gowns and suits which had been tested, some more successful than others. There was a sense of accomplishment in knowing she understood the material so that she could create viable clothing designs.

She entered Damien's office, and he looked up. "Con, my love. We have a visitor today, and I think this is an excellent opportunity for you to test the feasibility of your clothing designs."

Nothing could have surprised her more. "But... I thought it would be you dealing with the business side of things."

"My love, you are the best salesperson of the suits you've created. You know the positives of the material and if there are negatives which purchasers should know."

She stared at her father. "The negatives? Don't we just focus on what sells them best?" She was genuinely surprised by his comments, and she screwed up her nose, while trying to consider why they'd do that.

He smiled. "Constance, a good businessman knows that honesty is key. If those who order them know we'll tell them the full truth, then they'll return. It's just as important as the quality of the product. And we already know about that."

She considered his words, tossing them over. It does make sense, she thought. After all, she wanted those who purchased them to know that she'd created something of quality with the help of Laura, Lillian, and Sacha.

"Then what should I do, Damien?"

"If you're comfortable, then perhaps you should be wearing the suit you've created for yourself. It might be worth having a display of just how safe it is?" He smiled. "But only if you're comfortable with that idea?"

"You want to shoot me?" Constance blinked as realisation dawned. "You want to prove it to this man?"

"Matteo Bonita, yes. He's a good man, Constance, and he'll be shocked initially, but I think it will make understanding what the benefit of this item is, clear. He's..." Damien shook his head. "He's got ideas and plans, and there's danger ahead to achieve the destruction of his family house. I feel this product will assist his people."

Constance cocked her head. "You mean to do with taking down a SELED cell?"

His gaze narrowed. "What do you know about that?" Now his voice deepened, and lines crinkled at his forehead and around his mouth.

"I was aware of Frannie and Raphael's mission. I mean, they didn't tell me, but I'm old enough to know and hear. Besides, the staff do talk, especially when they don't realise you're there. It's amazing what you can learn. Wasn't that why I had to wait to leave here? Until your people found Raph's brother?"

"You're too curious for your own good, Con. Who knows that you know?" He spoke with an urgency that now had Constance frowning.

"I don't know? I mean, I wasn't overt about listening, but it's possible some saw me. And, of course, I guess some people might guess I know a little, given the ballista suit was created by me with Lillian, Laura, and Sacha's assistance."

A commotion sounded by the door, and Damien cleared his throat. "We'll have to finish this discussion later. Please go change into the suit, and I'll meet you by the testing building soon."

Constance's guts churned, and she considered his words as she rose. *Have I placed Damien, Ammy, and my family in danger?* She bit her lip as recriminations started cascading through her brain, and before she could turn the doorknob she turned back. "Did I do something really wrong?" She hated thinking she'd somehow welcomed the danger back into their lives. She dimly remembered leaving the big house in town. The men coming for them at the island.

She remembered the battered visage of Francesca when she'd returned with Raphael after she'd been kidnapped. *What have I done?*

Damien rose and stalked toward her, then enveloped her in a hug, the scent of cigar wrapping around her in a way she remembered from her childhood. Ammy and Damien had given her not just stability, but a family who loved her. They'd encouraged her to spread her wings, just as they had her brothers and sisters.

"I'm sorry, Damien."

"Oh, Constance, I'm sorry that you're going to be dragged into this mess. We'll talk later, I promise. Now go." He released her, opening the door, and she stepped away.

"Thank you, Daddy."

He blinked. "You haven't called me that in years, Connie love."

Matteo followed the young woman who'd come to find him from the hallway to what he guessed was an office, as another woman exited the room with her head down.

He only caught a flash of her face, but it was fine-boned, all porcelain skin with raspberry lips. He didn't catch her eye colour, but the silvery blonde hair was coiled upon her head in an ornate design. Her figure was svelte, and he noted that she wasn't tall, and determining her age was difficult. What he did know was that she looked like a fashion plate come to life.

Damien Whitmore waited by the door, watching the woman leave, staring after her until Damien noticed Matteo.

"Ah, Matteo, do come in."

They settled in the room after Damien shut the door. The armchairs of oak with burgundy leather sat before a fireplace, and the walls were lined with books. "Thanks for seeing me. I... Bloom sent me here, to discuss armaments for our proposed liberation of the island on which Casa Bonita stands."

"Yes, your father certainly built a fortress there, and I believe your brother has reinforced it significantly. He's also imported some interesting characters." Damien offered him a cup of tea.

"No, thank you. Yes, first Travis Haven, then later Edward Nobel and Alveraum Lores." He named the three men who had no interest in the rights of others outside the houses they'd assisted to descend into depravity. "My brother taking over makes it doubly dangerous, as he's not known for his interest in other's rights or safety and is... Let's just say, as the Master of Casa Bonita, he feels he may freely sample all on his radar." Matteo couldn't hide the fury in his voice.

Damien nodded. "That's what I'd heard. But tell me, is Lores still in residence?"

Matteo nodded. "I still have those inside who feed me information. They have said Lores is still there and has a fully functioning secure lab at his disposal. They can't tell me what he's working on, because he and my brother are sensitive to information leaks, but I believe there's something very large brewing. Before I left, the last time, I did get a peek at the arsenal they've been building, and it's..." He shrugged. "The things they're working on are of grave concern and include the enhancement of humans and flying craft with a fighting capacity. But that was over a year ago."

"Flying craft? How far advanced was that?" Damien leaned in, his face graven.

"Not far, I don't believe. There was no ability to keep the craft in the air for anything beyond a few minutes, and there's little space to afford a landing and take-off area," Matteo explained.

Steepling his hands, the older man seemed to consider what Matteo told him. "Tell me, what caused you to leave Casa Bonita?"

His guts knotted. "My sister. She was sent to Lores after an accident where she lost both an arm and a leg. He enhanced her, but not just her limbs. Other things as well. It changed her, and she became a..." His mouth dried just remembering the shell of his beloved Maria. "She wasn't herself. Didn't know me or others, did as she was told, but was stronger. Vicious. Maria had never been like that before, and that's when I realised my brother was dangerous, as was his drive to create a new world. One dominated by men with the same evil desires."

"Yes, I can see that would cause you great distress and make you question everything you knew. Well, I have things to show you." Damien drained his cup then laid it on the bench. "Follow me and we'll walk through my facilities, and I'll explain what we have and how we may assist you."

Matteo stood and waited as Damien grabbed a gun belt, slung it around his waist, and added two mean-looking pistols.

"You're expecting problems?" Matteo queried.

"Not exactly, but it pays to be prepared, Matteo. Now, come." Damien led the way as they opened and moved through the office door and down the expanse of hall, toward the very back of the house. "My wife and I settled in here many years ago, and it's allowed me to build and improve the structures which house my workplace. We have other manufactories too. Our daughter, Francesca Whitmore-Nobel, takes the lead on the manufacturing of the prosthetics with her husband and also heads up the Whitmore-Nobel foundation, while continuing her physiotraducere work," the man shared as they crossed the green lawn, headed for a large brick building. "My boys work in the manufacturing and..."

Matteo didn't realise that Damien had stopped until he almost ran into him. Damien had one of his pistols in hand, and pointed it at what Matteo thought was an intruder.

The whine of the pistol stunned Matteo, and he drew in a shocked breath. "Damien... What...?"

The figure in a grey suit turned, tugged aside a cloak just as Damien pressed the trigger again.

The person recoiled, and Matteo was moving as the figure fell to the ground.

Just as he reached the intruder, the person groaned, slid aside the cloak, and he realised it was a *she*! A small, slight figure, wearing a suit of shiny grey, which did nothing to hide the curves and dips of her body. Her face was hidden from view with a mask, but Matteo was sure when the whisps of golden hair escaped. Her fingers dug into the bottom of the mask lifted it.

"Damn it, Damien. You didn't even call out. I wasn't ready for you," she whispered.

"Constance, you're all right then?" Matteo didn't miss Damien's grin as the older man sank into a crouch and reached for the woman. He lifted her up so she was once more standing on her own two feet.

"Just bruised, but I did tell you that was likely to be the only wound. Unless you chose a head-shot." She shook out her gown and cloak. "Mr...?"

His gaze was captured by the most piercing gold and grey eyes he'd ever seen. "Miss Constance, I take it?"

She smiled, and her raspberry lips ticked up. "Yes. And I believe you are Mr Bonita?"

He shook his head. "Bonita was my mother's surname. I'm Matteo Garcia, though most call me Matteo Bonita, as that's Casa Bonita's title. It's a pleasure. I think." Then he rolled his eyes. "Well, maybe not a pleasure but—"

"I understand your meaning. Well, Damien. Are you satisfied with what you've seen? I told you it works. We tested it extensively in London before I returned home." Constance smiled at Damien, and Matteo's guts knotted again. There was just something about the woman. It could be the intelligence in her eyes, or the shape of those lips as they turned up in an impish smile...

Damien twirled a finger in the air. "Cape off and let me check you're all right."

The woman, Constance, sighed and followed his instructions. "See? It's all in the reinforced stitching of the material and the cut."

And the cut of the suit was perfectly moulded to her body, lovingly tracing the flare of her hips and the jut of her breasts... Matteo adjusted his stance, feeling an instant spark of heat deep in his loins.

"It's a pleasure to meet you, Mr Garcia... or Bonita." Constance held out a hand, and he glanced at it, took it. Wanted to raise it to his mouth but forestalled that instinct.

"The pleasure is all mine," he murmured.

Chapter Three

THE HEAT of a blush scorched Constance's face. She wanted to fan her skin but stopped herself. That gesture would be far too telling, and she'd learned much in the salons in London about the thrust and parry of coquetry. Not that she'd acted on it... No, that hadn't ever been in her plan.

"And you're here to..." she said.

Damien smiled at her as if she were a child he was indulging. She wanted to scream but kept the reaction deep within herself. She needed to prove herself an adult, a woman who was strong and capable, not the child he remembered so well.

"I'm here to discuss armaments with Damien." His voice was thick, like oozing molasses, and she wanted to melt into it. *An atypical response, Con. What are you doing?*

"Well, you're in the right place. Father has much which he and my brothers have invented—"

"And now your suit, my love. Come, change then bring it back for us to examine," Damien urged, and she wanted to remonstrate, but a seed of devilry raised its head.

"I'll be just a moment," she said, and sashayed away, aware that

Matteo Bonita's eyes were following, if the warmth infusing her limbs was anything to go by.

"Hey, Constance!" The sound of her brother's voice brought her up short, and she fought and failed to contain the blush. Turning around, she speared him with a glare.

"What?" She didn't look in the direction of Damien or Matteo but kept her attention on the doorway.

"I... Where do you want the trunk?" he mumbled.

"In the office. I need to go change," she said. "I'll be back in a few minutes," Constance added, then she scurried toward the house.

Matteo swallowed a smile as Constance left them. She was certainly sassy, and if he'd been free to consider a woman, well, he might just be tempted. But his journey was dangerous. He was the second son of the previous Master of Casa Bonita, and it fell to him to ensure the women and men who'd been subjugated were freed. And if that meant he'd have to give his entire future to achieve it... He'd do it. Besides—and now his grin died away—he wasn't unfamiliar with the darkness of humanity.

"She's amazing, isn't she? Just like my daughter Francesca, and in fact, all my children."

Matteo jumped in surprise and turned to find Damien watching him. "I apologise, sir..." he said stiffly, but Damien smiled.

"Nonsense. She's not my daughter of birth, but she's my daughter in my heart. Ammy and I adopted all five children after their mother died shortly prior to the Haven House uprising. From children without hope, they've created a future. Ammy and I are blessed."

Matteo understood what Damien was saying, that they all knew about darkness, but did Damien understand that Matteo wanted something more from her? That Matteo was interested in her sexually?

Is that what I am...? Matteo asked himself. No, Matteo realised, he'd misread the message when Damien continued. "They've all come so far. Francesca is a physiotraducere, Faith is an artist who creates sculptures of silver which are intricate yet beautiful, Sampson works with metals and designs the new armaments which round out the pickings in our arsenal. His skills surpass my own." Damien gave a laugh. "And Simeon? Simeon is a musician of note. You may have heard his sonatas? He's working with the ballet currently, writing a piece, in an ode to the President."

"They certainly seem to be over-achievers. You should be proud," murmured Matteo.

"Oh, I am. Haven House would have crushed them and lost the skills which improve our world." He shook his head. "Come, let's go through to the showroom and you will see what we have on offer."

He trailed the older man inside, his mind whirling with the information he'd just gleaned.

Constance hurried out of the suit. "Undo the top buttons and it loosens enough for me to remove the rest," she instructed her maid, Anna. Even as she was divesting herself of the fitted suit, she was directing Anna to pull out the loose pants and crisp white shirt she considered her work attire. "I'll need the black boots too," she added, now pulling on the pants with a sigh.

"Sir will be scandalised," Anna noted as she assisted Constance into the blouse.

"Nonsense. Father will see the value of movement, Anna. There now, grab those while I cinch in the waist." Her hands tugged on the ribbon of material, pulled it tight and secured it, before sliding her feet into the sculpted boots. Anna was hurrying to her knees with a boot hook in hand. "There has to be a quicker way to attend to this," Constance muttered, feeling the need to hurry in finalising her dressing.

Once Anna was finished, Constance swept up the suit and hurried to the door, aware of the time which had passed since she'd retired to change. What had Father shown Mr Bonita in that time? Had he explained the value of her suit? The journey she'd been on to create such an item?

She ran down the hallway and came to a speedy halt just outside the door, then swiftly scanned the area. No one had seen her helter-skelter rush, so now she had a moment, and she sucked in an unsteady breath before reaching out and opening the door.

The warehouse Damien called his showroom was cavernous, a large space which was lined and floored with highly polished surfaces.

"Papa, why did you decorate it like this?" the much younger Constance queried.

Damien smiled. "We might be selling armaments, but at its heart, what we do is part showmanship and part invention. Just because we deal in grease and oil and cogs, doesn't mean people don't expect to see it in a clean and professional environment. Remember that, my dear. If and when you work for me, these are things that will assist us to help people see us as professionals. Image is just as important as the quality. Never forget that."

The memory of that long-ago lesson wasn't lost on Constance now. Indeed, it was reinforced as she headed to the display Damien had insisted be prepared and laid out the skirt and jacket, beside the pants and suit coat she'd designed with her friends.

"Ah, just in time, Constance. Show us your designs." Damien's voice echoed, and she nearly jumped, glancing up to see them rounding the corner toward her.

"Oh, well, here we have the ladies' suit which, as you know, I wore earlier. And the men's. Each is tailored to fit the individual, ensuring the best possible coverage. No two suits are cut or fit the same, each is bespoke."

Matteo crowded in. "The fabric?"

"Designed in London by a new inventor, Lady Laura Canthrope, and her father. It's called ballistaproof, and I am the only accredited supplier of the fabric outside of England. Laura's father and I have an agreement, which doesn't allow anyone else to import the fabric, nor experiment with the substances from which it is engineered for the next ten years." She spoke with authority, knowing that the agreement would give her and Damien the breathing space to introduce it, and to ensure the knowledge wasn't used by others.

"Amazing," breathed Matteo. "And it's...?"

"Rated to hand profile ballistic use. Were someone to use a cannon... well, that is beyond the current specifications. Laura is working on improving the formulas, but for now, this offers protection from pistols and rifling. Of course, if say a panthera—our automaton fighting cats—were to attack, then it wouldn't offer appropriate protection, but that will require a higher level and that is being considered as we speak."

"But you mentioned the fit?" Matteo nudged.

"Oh yes, the fabric is dense, so it makes sewing and cutting a much more difficult proposition. I worked with others in London, and they designed a unit which allows me to machine sew the fabric and cutters that have a high tensile strength to cut through the layers which make up the garments."

"You can't just cut it?" Matteo asked, and Constance swallowed a laugh.

"No. Normal scissors don't have the power to cut properly, so we had to design something completely different to achieve that. It took years to perfect not just the cut and sewing, but also to amass the knowledge of the materials to achieve what we have here." She turned and smiled. "Here, feel the line of stitching, it's almost seamless. And the weight of the fabric, while heavier than wool, is still within the parameters of a comfortable weight."

She thrust the fabric into his grip, watched as he weighed it up, and noted the surprise on his face.

"Amazing," he muttered. "And how long does it take to craft something like this?"

Constance bit her lip. "Between the measuring, cutting, and sewing, which are slower than traditional methods, I can create a suit in around five days."

"Five days, huh? So how long to fit say, thirty?" His gaze narrowed. "And the cost?"

Damien cleared his throat. "As to that, we haven't yet finalised the cost to furnish a garment."

"How long? How long will it take you to come up with a pricing model?" His gaze was fixed on the suit, while his voice was firm. Demanding.

"I..." She looked at Damien, who frowned.

"I suppose, a few days. We'd need to cost the equipment, the imported fabrics and —"

"I want my men suited up. I need a price, Damien. And we'll need skilled sewers."

Constance cleared her throat. "There's only me." She shook her head. "So no one else would be capable of assisting—"

"You can teach others," Matteo suggested.

"No," Constance said firmly. "The contract we agreed to is clear. I am unable to teach anyone else for the first two years of the contract unless they are under my direct supervision, then only scale the business growth over the next five by no more than five assistants per year."

Matteo stared at her. "You're jesting, surely?"

She shook her head. "That's what I agreed to. It's part of the reason I hold the only importation license. Those are the rules, and I'm not going to bend or break them, Mr Bonita."

<h1 style="text-align:center">Chapter Four</h1>

DRESSING FOR DINNER, as Damien had insisted he stay, Matteo sighed. "It's been a long time since I dined with a lady, or a family for that matter," he muttered.

"Your late mother would be shaking her head over the state of your wardrobe," James Carrington, his assistant, said. "Back when you dined at the Casa, you had clothing to choose between."

"Yes, but I was also the second son, required to take multiple brides and breed up to build the strength of Casa Bonita," Matteo growled.

"Yes, well, now you have three decent suits and no building which she'd consider a home to speak of," James pointed out.

"I know. And even when we clear the mess, I still won't have much free coin or..." He shrugged. He wasn't looking to free Casa Bonita for the money or for the prestige with Bloom, but because it was the right thing to do.

But if you were to reclaim the fortune, you might be able to marry. Someone like Constance Whitmore would be—

Matteo cut off the thought, because he wasn't the kind of man a woman like Constance Whitmore deserved. She was young, and while she might have been touched by the darkness of Haven House, she was filled with a hope that would only be dimmed by him and his determination to end the scourge of SELED.

"Matteo?" James asked, and Matteo wondered how long he'd been caught up in the web of ifs and maybes.

"Wool-gathering." Matteo shrugged. "Well, I guess I should go down. You'll be fed?"

"The servants' dining room is almost as large and well-appointed as the one you'll be eating at. And I've been reliably informed that tonight the repast includes fricassee partridge and lamb meatballs."

Matteo smiled. "So, you won't starve. I shall leave you and head down to the parlour, James."

But he walked slowly, spending the time settling on how he was going to get the equipment he needed in an efficient manner. If he had to send his people here for fittings, the time lost would— "She needs to come with me, back to my headquarters." There was no other way around the situation. Time was of the essence; she needed to be with the men to ensure their suits fit.

By the time he'd stepped into the dining room, he'd committed to the course of action.

Tonight, Constance settled on a deep ruby red gown that sparkled subtly under the light of the chandelier. She knew it made her skin look creamy, and with a careful touch of rouge on her cheeks and a glossing of her lips, she looked ravishing, as Sacha had told her many times.

She'd taken a position beside the fireplace, fiddling with Faith's tiny soldiers when he entered the room. Constance knew it was Matteo, because her skin fairly prickled with awareness, zings of energy shot through her body. She took a moment, inhaling before she turned to face him.

Shock appeared on his face, his eyes widened, and his chest, the breadth of which was evident even though the careful cut of his suit appeared to minimise it, expanded and contracted with a rapidity which betrayed his apparent composure.

"Miss Constance." He bowed, and she was highly aware that for the moment they were the only two in the room.

"Mr Bonita," she returned and was surprised by the sudden deep timbre of his voice.

"You look quite fetching tonight," he said, and she noted the glitter of his grey eyes.

"Thank you, sir. Your suit is a Velmor, is it not? Of Highgrove Road?"

He nodded. "You know your tailors then?"

She shrugged. "During my time in London, my friends Sacha, Lillian, and Laura were most insistent that I should have more than a passing knowledge of tailors, modistes, and fabric purveyors."

The discussion suddenly felt like a dangerous dance of something she was barely knowledgeable of.

"Then I should thank them, I believe. You have only recently returned, I understand?"

"Yes, in the past two weeks. I was away for three years, honing my skills."

"You must have been barely fifteen when you left." He said the words with a smile which melted something inside her.

"Ah, you're smooth. No, I'm twenty-three. I was twenty when I left, as Father was concerned that I wait until it was safe... After Nobel Crest, things were fraught for some time."

Matteo winced. "Ah, yes. Since Edward Nobel went to Casa Bonita..." His words died away, and suddenly Constance felt stupid and mean. She hadn't intended to insult him.

"Forgive me. I didn't mean it like that. Francesca's husband, Raphael, was convinced there'd be a rallying of his troops, and he and Father went to great pains to round up those they could find."

His face became grimmer. "Except Edward Nobel. My apologies that he was offered succour at Casa Bonita. That was not my—"

"No! That wasn't what I meant at all," she said and shifted on her feet. "I spoke wrongly." She reached out, took his hand. "I meant no insult or disrespect."

"But it's true. My father and brother made an alliance. One that put your sister and her husband in danger. Your whole family, I believe. I apologise."

Before she could attempt to make a further apology, her father entered the room, Ammy on his arm.

"Mr Bonita, it's a pleasure to meet you." Ammy breezed forward, her left hand on the stick she only used during pregnancy, and it jolted Constance to think her adoptive mother was still young enough, and obviously able, to bear another child. Constance studied her adoptive mother's form as she reached with her right hand to make Mr Bonita's acquaintance and her lips curved up into a radiant smile. Yes, another babe is clearly on the way.

The others arrived and saved Constance from further embarrassment until dinner was served, and as she was the most senior unmarried woman, they were paired up to enter the dining room.

She allowed Matteo to take her arm, and she noted, again with surprise, a frisson of energy where they touched and the way her body responded, with unfamiliar heat. "I didn't mean to upset you, Miss Constance," he offered.

"You didn't, Mr Bonita."

"Matteo," he corrected. "Please call me Matteo."

Matteo watched the family interact at the table and damned himself for upsetting Constance. She'd been trying to make him feel at home, and he'd deliberately put a distance between them. He blamed the dress, the brilliant ruby washing over her skin, moulding to her breasts and hips.

Lust had speared him, and he'd wanted, and the only way to keep that at bay had been to seize upon her mentioning Nobel Crest. It had been far too efficient because she was stiff beside him.

"I apologise, Miss Constance," he said, glancing in her direction.

"You have nothing to apologise for. I spoke without thinking," she muttered, and he felt low, as her words betrayed her discomforture with the tiny stutter.

How the hell could he explain without going into detail he wouldn't share about himself? "I..."

"Now then, Mr Bonita. You've seen the facility my husband built. And you've seen the offerings. What are your thoughts?" Amaryllis Whitmore called from the head of the table, and he clenched one hand in a fist. He needed time, because something was urging him to save the situation before it spiralled out of his control.

"It's an excellent facility, and the range of offerings is truly amazing. I was hoping to talk to Mr Whitmore—"

"Damien," his host interposed.

"Of course, Damien, about my order. Bloom has graciously offered to underwrite our expenses until after Casa Bonita is liberated," Matteo said.

"Bloom has sent several potential customers in our direction. I like to think Whitmore Industries offers the widest range of equipment in the business," Damien explained.

"Indeed, you do. But you see, now that I've seen the ballista suit, my men would benefit from the offering. So much so, I need to order suits for all my senior officers."

Damien's eyes gleamed under the lighting. "And how soon would you be able to bring them here?"

"That's just it, Damien. That's not practical. It would be far more efficient for Miss Constance to return to my compound to create and fit the suits for my men."

Matteo felt her jerk and stiffen further beside him.

"I see. Yes, your point does make sense, however, we don't have the figures to price the suits yet. And Constance may not wish to travel with you," Damien pointed out.

"I understand that, but business is, after all, business, and the ballista suit would give my men an advantage. I need to ensure their safety. You want to advertise your product. I can assist with that while gaining the protection for my men. Come, Damien. This is business and—"

"Yes. On one proviso," Damien added.

"What? So long as it's within my means, I will certainly do my best," Matteo answered.

"You ensure the safety of my daughter."

Constance kept her gaze averted. Go to his compound? She so wasn't comfortable with that. Not after she'd botched her attempt to apologise. He must think her some kind of ham-fisted twit! Why do you even care? Between her shoulder blades, nerves twitched, just as they always did when she felt out of her depth.

The dinner finally ended, and while her parents were heading for the parlour, Constance took the opportunity to make her exit. "I'm feeling fatigued. I think I'll retire. Goodnight, all," she called, and she hurried from the room.

Being a coward wasn't her usual attitude, but tonight? It felt like she'd best ensure there was no chance of being alone with Matteo Bonita. He was handsome in a rough-hewn way, with grey eyes and chiselled features. A scruff of beard edged his jaw but did nothing to detract from the high forehead brushed with dark hair, that hinted at a curl. Nor did it detract from a fine patrician nose.

"And why have I even noticed all that?" she growled as she headed for her room at the far end of the hall, nearest the guest wing. As the family had grown, so too had the need to move bedrooms, and she'd been more than happy to negotiate a larger area, to allow for her to set up a workstation within what had once been a guest sitting room.

She stomped up to the door, had her hand on the knob when the sound of footsteps echoed. "Miss Constance? Please wait!" And there he was. Matteo Bonita striding toward her.

"I'm really tired," she said and faked a yawn, holding up a hand to her mouth.

"I... I didn't mean to be boorish. I must apologise." A red crest washed over his cheeks.

"It's fine, Mr Bonita."

"Matteo," he all but growled. "Please. I want to make sure you're comfortable, since we'll be sharing the compound."

Constance ground her teeth together, pasted on a false smile. "Oh, don't let my nerves get in the way. As you said, business is business, after all. When do we leave?"

He shook his head. "Ah, well, as to that..."

"When do you wish to travel to your compound?" She'd go, do her job, then return secure in the knowledge that once she began, it would take a freight train to move her from the appointed task.

"Uh, I'll be negotiating that with your father tomorrow, I believe. Miss Constance—"

"I really am fatigued," she responded. "Goodnight."

She fled into her bedroom, closing the door behind her then resting against it, feeling the hammering in her chest with a hand raised to her bodice. Eyes closed, she took a moment, inhaling, but the air around her felt like he'd invaded that. The scent of maleness—horses and cigar, wine, and him—surrounded her in an intoxicating cloud.

"No," she murmured. "Not him." She shook her head and stalked to the bed, fingers already plucking at the closure of her gown.

Chapter Five

MORNING DAWNED AND MATTEO ROSE, aware that in the bedroom next door lay a woman who intrigued him. One wholly out of reach.

She'd been frosty last evening when she'd demanded to know when they'd be leaving, and today, he'd be meeting with her father to arrange their business matters and their transport. If what she'd said was correct, she'd be residing on the compound for weeks, or even months. Close enough to learn many of his secrets, including the parlous state of his finances. To see the damage his father and brother had wrought.

"But it's worth it to have the suits," he muttered as he began washing.

James entered the room. "Morning, Matteo. What's your plan for today?"

"I'm meeting with Damien. Making arrangements, then we'll be off. Can you start packing up for us? I'm hoping this won't take long." He turned to focus on shaving, the razor sweeping away the stubble.

"I hear Miss Constance wasn't enthused with your conversation," James said, and Matteo's head nearly swivelled off his neck as he turned to look at his friend.

"What?"

"During dinner, apparently Miss Constance wasn't keen on conversation. The servants mentioned it last night at dinner." James frowned. "That's rather unlike you."

Matteo growled and cleaned up then rose. "I'm meeting Damien in a few minutes. Please, just focus on the task. We'll talk later." Then he stomped from the room, headed downstairs to the office.

Damien was waiting and invited him in, showed him to the seat near the fire, before closing the door. "I know I spoke yesterday about pricing, but I'm willing to cut you a deal. Once I have the costs from Constance, I give an undertaking to only add five percent markup. That keeps your costs low. I don't have a breakdown and may not have that for some time, however, you leave today. Take Constance with you."

"I'll send for Bloom's automotive—"

Damien shook his head. "No. You take my personal dirigible. Phoenix is fast, but she's also been outfitted with the newest armour plating and guns. Instead of you trundling along and being a sitting duck with my daughter on board, you're there in just over a day. I'm not trifling with my daughter's safety. You get that gratis. As I said last night, her safety is paramount. I will not send my daughter into danger."

"But negotiations—"

"The sooner my daughter is there safely, then back, the better for my peace of mind. I protect what's mine. I'll also send a personal guard with her, and that's not negotiable." Damien stood. "I'll be in touch with Bloom and will send you both the quotation and the invoice when details are hashed out."

"I..." Matteo considered the deal and knew what he was getting was far beyond what he and Bloom could have hoped for. "Thank you, Damien. I will guard your daughter with my life."

"You better, Matteo. Now go. Prepare and be on the way within an hour," Damien commanded.

Matteo rose, but before he left the room he turned and pinned Damien with a stare. "Why? Why are you sending us so quickly?"

Damien returned the look. "Because my intelligence says they know you're here. If they see you leave, they'll follow you, but leaving so quickly gives an element of surprise. I love my children—all of them—and I'll do anything to keep them safe. Constance isn't headstrong, but she's a dark horse. She'd go with you because she sees the benefit. If I told her not to go, she wouldn't, but she'd regret it and allow that to fester. I won't do that to her."

Matteo nodded and left the room.

Anna delivered the valise to her and began packing the trunk under Constance's eagle eye. "I need several pairs of the pants that look like skirts, and I'll likely need some skirts and blouses. Make that three, and two dresses. A wrap, my black cape. Oh! And I'd like the brown boots along with the black and the all-purpose shoes. A pair of slippers, match them to the dresses. No need to consider anything too dressy."

"You should add an evening gown, we can match it to your shoes, miss. You never know when you may need it. I've also added chemises, drawers, corsets, and nightwear." Anna sighed. "We should be able to get it all in one trunk if we pack carefully. Only I don't want to crush—"

"It's not a holiday, Anna. I'm there to work." Constance stomped over to her desk and scooped up the patterns she had worked so hard to make, turned to the maid and nodded. "I'll need all the material, the composite threads, and sewing machine. Oh yes! And the powered cutting utensils and white marking pencils." The maid scurried off to fulfill the list of requirements while Constance filled a smaller valise with her diary and toiletries that were essential before Anna returned to the room.

"Miss, the master said we needed to be ready within the hour." Anna was moving with haste, folding the clothing and filling the trunk. "He's sending Anderton with you, as a guard."

That stopped Constance in her tracks. "A guard?"

Anna nodded. "Anderton has been recalled from the manufactory, and I saw the armaments and ammunition he's sent ahead to the Phoenix."

"Why would he...?" The Phoenix was Damien's personal speedy, armed dirigible. It had been custom made with help from Sampson, while Faith had assisted with the design of the craft. It was fast, heavily fortified, and while it could only hold a dozen or so passengers, the size didn't bely the luxury within.

"I heard that it was because you would be travelling, and as a Whitmore, the master was concerned you'd be a target."

The family had faced these kinds of dangers before, and now she understood the implication. When you understood that, and the fact that the work was for Bloom, it all made sense. Even though the teams who worked for the man were essentially unknown by most, those in the families who were touched by the SELED group were taught about the dangers, especially after Francesca's ordeal, and took all necessary precautions.

Ammy had been incandescent with rage that her daughter, Francesca, was wholly unprepared for the danger, and Ammy had personally torn strips off the now-elderly Bloom after Francesca's abduction. Ammy had made it clear that such danger was unnecessary, and he'd acquiesced with certain caveats. The biggest was no discussion about Bloom's anti-SELED movement outside the household.

So, Faith, herself, and their younger siblings were educated about SELED, the dangers, and were closely protected. When appropriate, they were also instructed on various forms of martial arts and small ballistic armaments, including pistols. It was one of the things she'd nearly forgotten in London. Nearly. Except for the work she'd undertaken for her father in a covert fashion, learning about the ballistaproof fabric, that was. Apparently, he had heard whispers, and when she'd been allowed to finally travel, he'd requested she make enquiries. Thankfully Raphael's cousin had put her in contact with the people she'd needed to meet.

"Chance is a funny thing," she told herself.

"Sorry, Miss Constance?" Anna asked.

"Nothing," she answered. "Is everything ready?"

Anna nodded.

"Good. Let's send for a man to load it onto the Phoenix. Then I suppose I best go say goodbye to Ammy and the others."

Once Anna had left, Constance inhaled deeply. It was as if something momentous was about to happen, as the nerves in her belly quivered. She hadn't felt quite so... discommoded on leaving here before, or even London. Why now? It was a question she didn't have an answer for.

When the rap came at her door, letting her know it was time to say goodbye and leave, she was sure she was making a life-altering decision, and it was one she wasn't totally comfortable with.

The small dirigible was humming as Matteo made his way up to the landing dock. The craft was sleek, a shiny bronze and heavy-duty material craft. The bubble holding the cabin rose up into the air, and the cabin was dark wood, polished to a high shine. On the side he saw the painting of a phoenix in flight, trails of fire flying behind it.

"She's a beauty, isn't she? We took delivery of her after Constance left, so this will be her first journey on the Phoenix. It's actually the second dirigible I own called the Phoenix." Damien indicated that Matteo should precede him into the cabin area. "There's a full kitchen, five bedrooms for travellers, and the required amenities. There's also a cabin for the captain, and a bunkroom for the men. There's sufficient hydrogen to power it for a week aboard the balloon. I've also had the latest communications equipment fitted on board, and in the holds, there are three pantheras, and an automotive machine. It's a special one with an exoskeleton, so it can be locked down if necessary. Armaments include three cannons, an actinic ray, and the men are highly trained warriors too."

Matteo was amazed at how much was packed into the tiny craft. "And the weight...?"

"The balloon has a capacity to handle up to three times the weight placed on it, and we can swap out the cabin if necessary, however, I have alternative dirigibles, so..." Damien shrugged.

"I will protect Constance for you, Damien."

"You will indeed. She's my daughter, not of my body, but she was young when Ammy and I married and took on the children. Like Francesca, I feel so strongly that she's mine. If anyone hurts so much as a hair on her head, I'll kill them. I would do that for any of my children, Matteo. Remember that." Now he nodded as if he'd imparted something he needed to share, and Matteo felt the words all the way to his soul.

"I won't let anyone near her, Damien."

"Then we both understand where we stand." Damien smiled. "Now, here she comes. I'll wish you both a safe journey." He stepped away, and Matteo turned to see Constance striding toward him, dressed in the strange skirt that appeared to split in the middle, then he realised they were pants.

The captain, who'd been hovering near the doorway to the cabin, hurried forward. "Miss Constance. Mr Bonita." He nodded obsequiously. "Welcome aboard the Phoenix. Mr Whitmore was most emphatic we should get you there as quickly as possible, so the most direct route is the one we'll take. Miss Constance, your guard is already on board and has checked the cabin and balloon to ensure your safety. Let's get moving. If you'd like to come forward to the wheelhouse, and watch as we lift off?"

Matteo was intrigued enough to want to, but he waited for Constance to agree with, "That would be interesting," before he agreed as well, with, "Yes, that would be most enjoyable."

She filed in behind the captain, and they moved forward. Looking through the large windows, Matteo could see Damien had moved beyond the platform and watched as the burly men untied the ropes which kept the dirigible on the ground before they swarmed aboard.

"My men are very well-trained," the captain explained. "Each hand-picked. In a worst-case scenario, they are trained across a broad range of roles, so we can do most of the tasks required," the man boasted.

"Indeed." Isn't it amazing what money can achieve? Matteo wasn't bitter, but from time to time, he wished he had access to the resources of Casa Bonita to facilitate his role in bringing it down.

Matteo watched as Constance took a seat near the console where the captain hovered, his hands settling on the wheel. "Time to rise!" the captain called, and suddenly there was the sensation of them leaving the ground. Air whooshed around the cabin, and the whomp, whomp, whomp of whatever the part was called, was turning, and started to propel them forward as they rose toward the clouds.

Chapter Six

CONSTANCE WAITED BY THE WINDOW, watching the land speed away beneath her. The evening meal was being prepared, the scent filling the ship, and she inhaled as she contemplated how this had happened.

Here she was, speeding somewhere unknown, on her way to making a collection of suits for men she didn't know, to assist in the freedom of another house. "How do Ammy and Francesca do it?" The words echoed as she considered the situation.

She wasn't a fighter like her sister or adoptive mother. She was trained, true, but it had never been her dream to be part of this world. Instead, she'd focused on something she loved! She'd learned from her sister as a young girl, the process of sliding a needle through material and creating something. That had always been her safe place. That focus had helped her come to terms with her history, memories, and the nightmares she'd fought in the passing years.

Her vague memory of her mother, a pale shadow cared for by Francesca, was all she really remembered of the woman who'd given her birth, but she remembered the voices, the sounds. The pain.

She contained the memories well, but sometimes they leaked when she was stressed, like she was today.

Her fingers dug deep into the sills of the windows.

Would she dream tonight? Would the nightmares she worked so hard at controlling make their way into her brain? The hot burn of her eyes warned her that her grip was tenuous.

The sound of a door opening told her that someone had entered the room. The scent of him? That told her who it was. *Matteo Bonita.*

He was an enigma. He appeared controlled, but she suspected there were depths that he hid. He might seem self-contained, but she had a suspicion he was frustrated that he needed the assistance of others, men such as Bloom, to facilitate what he felt driven to complete. What else was hidden beneath the mask she was so sure he wore? He was smooth, debonair even.

"Miss Constance, I believe the meal is about to be served." He spoke clearly, his voice smooth and dark, but it was the heat of him that warned her of his nearness. Against her better instincts, she wanted to be close, to feel the heat that emanated from him.

"I... Yes, of course." She turned, carefully avoiding his gaze as she made her way to the door.

"Miss... Constance?" His voice betrayed confusion.

"Yes?" She inwardly cursed the husky sound of her voice.

"Is there... Are you well?"

"Yes. Merely hungry," Constance answered, more than a little aware that she was lying to him. She wasn't well. She'd never really been well. A better description was that she'd coped. "Now, show me to the dining room." She swept from the room, blinking rapidly, attempting to control the physical indicator of her concern.

His hand found her elbow, stilled her. "Constance?"

She sighed, raised her head. "Yes?"

"What's wrong?" He frowned, and she had this mad urge to lift her hand and cup his cheek. Clenching her fists helped her to control that.

"Nothing. Thank you for your concern, Mr Bonita."

"My name is Matteo," he growled. "You're going to be seeing a lot of me, so you might best start calling me that."

She blinked. "Mr Bonita—"

He laughed, the sound harsh. "I get you don't like me, Constance. But for the benefit of my people, please. My name is Matteo. Use it."

"I don't dislike you," she answered, stung by his words. "I don't know you well enough to make that kind of decision."

"Right. Fine. You tell yourself that, but Constance, we're going to be in close quarters. The men call me Matteo. Bloom calls me Matteo. So will you. Get used to it. Now we should go into dinner." He let her go and the loss of heat was a shock to her system. It took a moment for her to realise she should follow, then she did.

The meal passed in near silence, but Matteo wasn't enjoying it. He hadn't meant to be so severe with Constance, but a primal instinct in him had risen, noting the way she appeared so fragile, her fingers digging into the wood, as if she were holding on for dear life.

Then he'd requested she call him Matteo, and he'd fought hard when she'd refused and instead called him Mr Bonita. She didn't know how much he detested that last name. He could make her use Garcia, but with the grip of Casa Bonita, that was really how he needed to be known.

Two generations degrading the name made it hard to bear, along with the knowledge of the women and children who had no option, in either name or living a life that degraded them. The SELED group made women little more than sexual slaves and chattels to use as the men saw fit.

After Maria had been given to Lores, there had only been one other sibling he was close to. His little sister, Nadia, had also been consumed by the squalid life, and it consumed her sunny nature until she was angry. He hated that for her, and memories of how broken she'd appeared after her 'marriage' haunted him.

"Mr... Matteo, I'm sorry. I'm not very good company today. I think..." She raised a hand to her brow. "I think I should go lie down." She rose, and when he started to do the same, she shook her head. "No. Finish your meal. I just... Some days I have a migraine." Then she swept from the room.

He frowned down at the meal. It was lovely. Fresh and well-cooked. The wine exquisite, and yet she'd barely touched her food, and for him it was now like eating ash. He pushed away from the table, placing the napkin on his plate. "James? Meet me in my cabin. I've things to discuss with you."

His friend made to put down his knife and fork and Matteo felt a spurt of self-aimed anger. "No. You finish first, then we'll meet. I've some things I need to attend to before."

He left the room and strode down the corridor toward his cabin, next to Constance's. The closer he drew, the louder a noise came. Sobbing.

"Damn it!" he growled, knocked on her door, then shoved inside.

She was hunched on the bed, face raised toward him with surprise. "I..."

"I knew something was wrong, Constance." His guts churned with fury. *Who the hell made this beautiful woman so sad? Who left her sobbing?* His fists curled into tight balls. "Constance?"

"I... I hate this world. I hate the Houses who control it." The fury and loss on her face tore at him.

"Why? What happened, Constance? Who hurt you?" He stalked forward then crouched beside her. "Let me help you."

Her hand clenched a handkerchief, and he watched as she visibly reined in her distress. "You can't. He... They've already been dealt with." But even though she pulled the emotions within her, in her eyes he could still read the shadows of pain. He wanted to soothe her, banish the darkness...

He shook his head.

"Matteo, sometimes... There are times when the pain just comes up and grabs me. I think things happened so fast, and I didn't have time to prepare myself. I just..." She shrugged. "Sometimes it just sneaks up on me."

"You don't have to face it alone." *Hypocrite.* Since when was he a soft ear to listen, and when did he follow that advice himself?

"No. I know that." Her voice strengthened, and he understood the implicit request for him to leave. So, he rose, backed away.

"Constance, I'm here, and if I can assist, you only need to ask." Then he left the room, closing the door with a quiet snick.

Even as he headed for his cabin the words he'd spoken, the promise he'd made, swirled around in his head.

Night had fallen and Constance huddled on the chair by the window, looking out into the night sky. The sound of the engine of the dirigible was the only sound as everyone else had retired. Beside her a small light shone, banked so that it did little more than banish the darkest aspect of the night.

She shivered, dragging her wrap closer around her body, covered only by a fine lawn nightgown.

The journal she'd kept since her tenth Christmas was laid on her lap, the pen in her hand, and she looked down.

Matteo was very kind today. I believe he saw that I was in pain.
Did I try hard enough to hide it? Was there some tell or action
that betrayed me?
I don't know what to do.
I know the world isn't a kind place, and I know I'm lucky. I have
Damien and Ammy and the rest of my brothers and sisters. But
the memories of those who weren't so lucky haunts me. I remember
Mama and the pain of when she died.
I remember the sounds of pain when she was brutalised and made
to do things she didn't want to. I remember the threats and the
way he made her pay. I remember the things I saw, heard. And
the things that he did to us. They echo in my brain.
I can't run fast enough to hide from those memories, and that
slices through me.
I can't sleep, because if I do, the demons of my past will revisit me.
I know they will, even though I'd thought I'd finally defeated
them.
I have no choice but to stay awake until we land. Until I find
somewhere safe, where no one will hear me.
I'm so tired of this. I'm tired of the pain and the fear.

When will this end?

Condensation covered the glass where she breathed, as she sat there considering the words she'd written. The journal itself was such a strange thing. Every time she was in a position she couldn't handle, she'd taken to writing it down in the book, letting the pain flow onto the page. The paper and leather item absorbed her pain and fears in a way she'd never be able to explain to others.

However, the book also contained the secrets she desperately wanted to shy away from.

"I can't let this destroy me. I am stronger. I will overcome these memories and create a safer future for myself." The words, like an affirmation, grounded her. Let her look forward, so she could craft hope that better days and memories would eventually swamp out the fear.

Realising that she needed to move, needed to keep herself active, she reached into the valise and tugged out the sewing bag she'd stashed within it.

The fabric she was working on was a piece she'd been working on for years. The material fine silk and the skein of cream that she threaded in the low light almost glowed. She glanced at the wild rose she was embroidering, which was merely one of the flowers she'd planned to embroider on the material. The bouquet of white lily, wild rose, daisy, honeysuckle, and tulip would be a message to her younger sister Faith, for the day she would give her hand in marriage. Each flower had a meaning: devotion, pure love, pleasure and pain, and true love.

Her hands began to move with slow and sure strokes, and as she worked, her emotions settled, and soon somnolence rose, but she thrust it aside.

Chapter Seven

THE GROUND ROSE UP, and the ropes were thrown out as men gripped on and jumped to the ground. The sounds of the engine slowed as the cabin touched the earth. In the distance was the small township Matteo called home.

It wasn't well-off, and some might even call it down-at-heel, but it suited his needs, given its location was only hours from a major settlement. The traffic-way of commercial dirigible systems afforded him a quick and easy way to travel from location to location, and yet, that little extra distance had ensured the land he'd needed to purchase, hidden from view by high trees and defensible due to its high location, had been affordable. His funds were limited, though he'd been very careful with his investments.

The blue of the lake in the distance glittered in the early morning sun, and he breathed deeply, letting the clear air fill his lungs.

"It's good to be home, Matteo," James said.

"It is indeed, and I'm sure Lana will be pleased to see you," he added with a grin.

James blushed deeply. "Lana and I don't have any understanding…"

"Then you two are the only ones who think that. Everyone is waiting for one of you to make a move, James." He shrugged on his coat, as the cool air was a shock after the warmer climate of the Whitmore ranch.

Footsteps, light and quick, echoed in the hall, and he turned, waiting for Constance to join them. Her face was pale, her eyes shadowed, yet the sadness that had almost swallowed her yesterday was nowhere in sight. *You can hide from it, and hide it, but it's still there.*

"Good morning, Constance," he said, holding out his hands.

He noted the flare of surprise followed by a small smile. "Good morning, Matteo. James." She nodded to them one by one, and Matteo returned the smile.

"Good morning," James muttered then moved away, shoving his hands into his pockets. "I'll make sure the bags are ready for transport. Round up some to assist us to transport the trunks."

Constance watched his retreat. "Did I say something...?"

"No. He's just feeling a little needled. I mentioned the young lady he's sweet on and who's sweet on him. He's... We men who leave the houses sometimes struggle to make the first move toward women. We fear coming across as demanding total obedience, so sometimes we are too soft. Take too long."

"Raphael isn't like that," she answered.

Matteo barked a laugh. "No. Raphael is a force of nature. Maybe we need an infusion of that in our ranks."

"Perhaps," Constance said with a laugh. "But maybe that's because he's perfect for Frannie. She's direct enough that anything less might get lost."

"I've not met your sister. The last time Raphael and I were in the same room was just after the birth of their first child."

Constance laughed. "James Damien Whitmore-Noble. Quite a mouthful really."

"Indeed. I got the Damien, but James?" he queried.

"Oh, her father and mine were different. James was her father, and I believe he was a good man. One who refused to take another wife. When he died, our mother was parcelled off to someone who was a true believer. That was our father." She shrugged, but Matteo noted the frailty that she exhibited during the action. "He wasn't a pleasant man."

"You remember him?"

"Oh yes," Constance answered. "You don't forget someone like that easily. Anyway, I take it this is your home?"

It was impossible to miss that she wanted to end the topic of conversation, and he chose to agree. "Yes, Bald Head is nice. It's free of the taint of SELED. My people live on a compound but interact fully with the community. We see it as our responsibility to ensure the needs of those who are met. We built a community hall and the church. The few children from the compound attend the local school, and in the future, we'd like to assist to build the community. It needs more houses so our families may relocate into town, find employment while feeling safe. I intend to be more involved once the threat is past."

"Why? Why have you done this?" She turned to face him. "You know the dangers..."

"We do. But unlike the houses, we need to assimilate into society. We want our children to have a future. So, we see it as our responsibility." He wondered how much more he should share, but for now, maybe less was a better option.

"I see," she answered. "I... I must go collect my valise." And she almost sprinted away, into the hallway.

The captain came into the parlour. "Well, safe and sound as I promised Mr Whitmore. The men are gathering the items from the hold."

"James has been instructed to find a carriage for the goods. And—"

"Mr Whitmore gave instructions that the pantheras and automotive are to be placed at your service. The automotive should allow you to make the journey to your home in grand style." The captain bobbed his head, and it annoyed Matteo. The man was like a lapdog, panting with excitement in a way that Matteo found unprofessional and teeth-grindingly saccharine. The saving grace, he supposed, was that he must be an exceptional dirigible captain.

"Yes. Thank you."

Constance joined him now, and he was both pleased and grateful. "Come, here is James with a wagon, and the automotive is being unloaded."

"Of course." They moved to the open doorway and out onto the deck. Men waited to open the side and they stepped onto the plank and made their way down to the platform.

The automotive drove up before them, and he thanked the heavens he had previous driving experience. The vehicle was long and sleek, the copper and brass exo-structure gleamed, and the symbol on the side was the Whitmore coat of arms, and at some thirty feet long, he was sure they wouldn't feel crowded.

James stepped up. "It's a very beautiful vehicle. I believe it's got the equivalent of thirty horsepower and is apparently powered by a petroleum distillate engine."

The front was elongated and decorated in silver, with three prancing unicorns sculpted in silver adorning the hood. The eight wheels were topped with copper covers, decorated with intriguing leaf designs, and the cabin of the vehicle was lush, with two exquisite rows of black leather seating which reminded him of the armed chairs within the Phoenix itself. The engine hummed gently, and inside the steering panel was copper again, gleaming and covered with the same black leather as the seat covers. Knobs and switches worked aspects of the machine. As they climbed within and the door shut, the engine was almost silent.

Matteo settled into the piloting seat, and Constance took the seat beside him while Anderton climbed into the back. "Have you driven an automotive like this before?"

He frowned. "Not quite like this." He ran his hand over the embellishments, still surprised by the hidden aspects of the exo-structure Damien had told him about. He wondered how it would unfold to protect the vehicle.

She nodded. "I have only a few times, but this one is very simple to pilot." She pointed to a button. "This one is the forward propulsion, and this one," she said, pointing to another, "is backward."

"And the throttle?" He felt like a fool.

She smiled, took his hand, and slid it onto a small knob. "Turn to the right to speed up and left to slow down."

"And to stop it?" Matteo asked.

"There's a button on the floor, press that slowly and keep pressing until we stop," Constance explained.

He turned the knob very slightly, then depressed the forward button and the automotive slid forward.

Constance sat back in the seat and closed her eyes. "I forgot how much Father likes his comforts," she murmured. "This one is new, but I really like it."

He steered the vehicle slowly onto the gravel roadway and wondered at how well-sprung this was; the ruts didn't jostle them, and as he increased the speed, the vehicle maneuvered along until they were soon at the gates of the compound.

Anderton climbed from the car. "I'll get the gates open, then we can enter, and I'll wait out here until the wagon arrives."

As the gates opened Matteo looked at Constance, waiting to see what she thought as they drove into the well-guarded yard. "Welcome to my home," he said.

Constance didn't quite know what she expected, but it certainly wasn't this. The houses were well-cared for, gardens full of vegetables, and flowers brightened the central zone while children ran and played, and women hung washing out on long lines.

"How many live here?" She leaned toward him as the vehicle inched forward.

"At the moment, we have about one hundred and fifty. The numbers ebb and flow as men come, bring their families, and use it as a sort of halfway house arrangement."

"Halfway house?" She didn't know the term.

"A kind of point halfway from a SELED house to freedom. Many need help learning skills which will allow them to find a way in society, to start the education of their children, and to gain the skills which will help them find work. We do that here, as well as the men forming an armed force to work toward freeing the residents of Casa Bonita and other houses."

Now she looked at him in a totally different light. "You really want to help more than just those from Casa Bonita? I..." Matteo stopped the car and they all alighted while she thought back over the years.

Damien had helped her family, along with others who'd escaped Haven House. Then with Raphael, they'd been there for Nobel Crest, but usually the assistance to individual house refugees was organised in an *ad hoc* manner.

She considered the man before her. "And you've personally paid for all this?"

He shrugged. "I had more than them, but the resources are limited. We try to do what we can with what we have. Anyway, you should come inside. I need to contact Damien, let him know we've arrived safely."

She followed Matteo into the nearest structure, a shed, but within she was surprised, as it had been converted to a living space. "That's different."

"I needed to house families, so the main house has been sectioned up, with bedrooms shared by families, the kitchen doubles as a work-space to teach the women how to make meals, to prepare foods for storage and still produce food for the workers. We've erected more housing on-site, but this..." He shrugged. "My needs were less, so we converted this, made it big enough to house myself and guests. There's three bedrooms, a small kitchen and living area. The rest of this building is a work area, offices, and storage."

It was efficient, clean, and well-cared for. The furnishings weren't new or opulent, but they spoke to her in a way she couldn't have expected. He opened one of the internal doors. "This bedroom will be yours. There's just us here, and your guard will be housed with the single men. There's bunk-style accommodation for them behind this building, so he's close enough."

Constance nodded and looked at the room. A large tester bed, with a small wardrobe, chest of drawers, and washing facilities. "And the bathroom?"

"The room next door," he said and pointed to the wall to indicate which side. "Now, the communicase is in the living area, so if you'd like to come through and..."

Constance shook her head. "No. I'll unpack first. Then you and I can see where I'll set up my workspace if that suits you?"

"Of course." He bowed. "I'll have your trunk sent in when it arrives." Then he left her, shutting the door with a soft snick.

Chapter Eight

MATTEO DISCONNECTED from the communicase transmission and glanced in the direction of Constance's door. She wasn't like any other woman he'd ever met. He'd almost expected her to decry the accommodation and had been prepared to clear one of the suites at the large house for her use, but instead, she'd accepted the space, requested a work area, and had made no real demands.

He, like others, knew some of her background. Hell, the story of her family was practically famous. The saving of Amaryllis Whitmore by the dashing ranger, Damien, had been written and re-written. The tale fictionalised and shared in newssheets, and even Francesca and Raphael's story had been covered extensively. But they had gone on to live in comparative luxury. He'd seen it for himself, the house splendid with chandeliers and servants.

She'd never settle for the likes of me.

"Where the hell did that come from?" he muttered, then he turned as the sound of footsteps echoed behind him.

"Where did what come from?" James queried.

"A random thought, my friend. Any trouble on the way here?" Matteo scanned James' face.

"Nothing. It's all very quiet in a strange 'I think something is building' sort of way." James scratched his head.

"It's been quiet for too long," Matteo agreed. "But I need to find a workspace for Miss Whitmore and—"

"She's not what I expected," James offered.

Matteo's chest seized. "What do you mean? Why is she not what you expected?" An unfamiliar emotion pushed him to ask.

"Well, she's not snotty or bitchy. She's welcoming and seriously beautiful." James' face turned in the direction of the bedroom door. "I... She's quite a nice woman, actually."

"She's here to work, James, and when the task is complete, she'll go home to her nice house, and her nice family, and find a nice man to marry." He spoke with a touch of bite and noted that James' eyes narrowed.

"What—"

The door opened in time with James' speaking.

"So, where shall I work? I'll need space, and something for people to stand on. A table or two." She'd removed the cape, her hat, and had somehow done something with her hair so it was looser, framing her face. Then she looked from Matteo to James and back to Matteo again. "Oh, I'm sorry. Do you want me to..." She waved at the door.

James smiled, and it was softer than Matteo remembered. He smiled too but was sure it was thinner and strained. "No. James and I were just discussing the trip. He'll have your trunk brought in and—"

"Oh, that's wonderful. It's the blue one. The others are red and will need to be transported to my work area, wherever that is?" She smiled, and for some reason, Matteo thought it was like the sun was shining on him.

"There's a space in the building here. I'll take you there while James checks in with the guards, arranges accommodation in the bunkhouse for your man, and—"

"Of course." James bowed low. "I'll see you later, Miss Whitmore."

"Constance," she called at his retreating back. "Well then, let's find this area, shall we?"

He didn't miss the twinkle in her eye. "You like to sew?"

She grinned. "It's honest work, I'm creating something new, and yes, I do enjoy it. But tell me," she said and leaned in, "do the ladies here know how to sew? Is it something they might wish to learn while I'm here?"

He blinked, not expecting that at all. "I... I don't know."

She nodded. "No disrespect, but men don't usually consider these things. If the ladies know how to sew, they can make their children's clothes, mend them. And if their work is good enough, they may be able to work in the home, sewing and mending for others."

"I'll discuss it with my house staff. But for now, come this way." He led her to another doorway. "This leads through to the work zone. I... It makes sense for it to be close so..."

She nodded. "Yes, I can see that it would. Damien likes the warehouse to be close too." Constance followed him through the door and into a narrow hallway.

"There's an empty office in here," he said as he opened a door. The room wasn't very big, but it was private.

Constance frowned, chewed her lip. "It's not really very big."

"Not big enough? Or...?"

"I'll need light, and two tables at least. A dais, and a way to hang completed garments. It's just..." She shrugged. "But if it's all you have...?"

He sighed. "My office is much bigger, but you'd have to share, I'm sorry." He strode to the end of the hall. His space had extra tables for laying out maps, chairs enough to hold meetings of the men in change of their campaign.

"Oh," she said. "I can get noisy sometimes. The machine is mechanical." Constance appeared concerned as she sucked in her lower lip, and it made his body react, the increased heartbeat, heat suffusing his body along with other inconvenient indicators.

Matteo growled, cleared his throat, and shoved his hands deep into his pockets. "I can ignore it," he said and waited as she entered the room.

Her gaze ran over the area, up to the windows, and she appeared to consider the space. "I'll need a stand, but yes, I can work in here." And she nodded and he knew he had a problem.

Constance hovered, watching as the precious trunks were carried into the area where she would work. She opened each, inspecting the contents, and when the sewing machine emerged, she sighed, reached in, and grunted slightly as she raised it.

"Here, let me." And there was Mr Bonita—Matteo, as he'd reminded her to call him—and he grabbed the machine without effort. Now he waited for her to indicate where she needed it placed.

"Thank you," she said, feeling strangely aware of the man.

Since their conversation about his halfway house. Learning that he was using his limited financial resources to fund this compound, she looked at him... not quite differently, but perhaps with a new lens. Many of the men she'd met both in America and England had been interested in presenting themselves in the best possible light. Everything they did, with the exception of Raphael and her father, had been to make themselves appear more interesting or trustworthy. But sadly, she'd watched and found that to be skin deep. Not what she looked for in a man.

Matteo appeared to walk his own path.

Casa Bonita had funds aplenty, but like many second, third, and subsequent sons of the masters, those funds were centralised to the heir apparent.

"Matteo, may I ask...?"

"What, Miss Constance?"

She rolled her eyes. "My name is Constance, not Miss Constance. If I call you Matteo, then you call me Constance, yes?"

As he nodded, she inclined her head toward the yard. "I was wondering how you came to have the funds to make all this happen." It was forward, the question, but she desperately needed to know more. And that desperation stemmed from something she didn't understand either.

"Ahh... That's complicated. You know a little about Casa Bonita? The money is central to the house, yes? So, I always knew I'd need to find alternative cash flow. In the years before I left the house, from the time I was fifteen, I ran a business of my own. My education was ended early because I wasn't the heir, so learning to fish seemed an obvious choice. The elderly man who'd fished for Casa Bonita had died and there was a gap or need. I like time outside and prefer to work with my hands." He raised them, looked down.

She noted that they weren't soft but scarred and worn. She... She liked that. A man willing to make himself.

Her mouth dried as she reached out, took his hand. "That's a wonderful thing, Matteo. That you worked so hard that you could afford..."

He laughed. "Ah, no, that gave me seed money. I invested it from there, learned how to make money with money. I kept fishing until I left the house, grew my stake and my investment grew too." He shook his head. "I'm not rich but..."

"Your money was gained honestly. I... I like that, Matteo." She blushed, the heat burning the skin of her face, but she refused to raise her hands to hide her cheeks.

The air around them thickened, and the racing of her pulse warned her that she should move away.

But her body swayed toward him. His hands moved up her arms, to her shoulders. Was it to steady her or something else?

His eyes deepened in colour, and the whisper of his breath on her lips had her eyes closing.

"Matteo! Matteo!" James' voice broke through the veil that surrounded them, and she lurched away, as if she'd been slapped.

"What?" Matteo swung away, and she felt strangely abandoned.

"I've just got word. Your brother? He's had an accident." James entered the room, face flushed.

"What?" Matteo stiffened.

"Javier, he's been hurt. There's chatter that he's in a serious condition. I've got people trying to find out what we should know."

"Damn," Matteo growled. Then he turned. "I beg your pardon, Constance."

She waved a hand, because she was sure he felt concerned for his brother's welfare.

"We need to find out what happened. How severe his injuries are. We need to know if that will give us some kind of advantage," Matteo added.

His words surprised Constance. "But he's your brother—"

Matteo shook his head. "My brother, the person I knew, died long ago. This Javier is an ugly and dangerous person. He would kill anyone to retain control of Casa Bonita. James, put the men on notice. Start gathering our equipment. Constance," he said and turned to her, "how quickly can you have suits made?"

She shook her head. "It's not quick. I mean, I can possibly have one or two ready in a couple of days, but that's working every hour."

"Start with James'—"

James shook his head. "No. Yours should be first, Matteo. They'll come for you over—"

"Nonsense," Matteo said.

She waited and considered. Both the men were of similar size and proportions. "I can take your measurements today. Both of you. Have the pattern redrafted maybe tonight and begin cutting the cloth. It's the sewing that takes days, but I'd need you both available for fitting sooner rather than later."

Matteo's brows drew together. "I... All right then. What do you need?"

"I need to set up here first. Give me an hour, then I'll be ready. Matteo, you first, then James."

Matteo nodded. "I'll come back in an hour then."

Both men exited the room, and she sat there, still shell-shocked at what she'd learned in the last ten minutes.

Matteo seemed to have little concern for the well-being of his brother. She couldn't understand that; if Faith or Francesca or any of her siblings were injured or ill, they'd all rush to the other's side. But clearly Matteo didn't feel the same. Why?

The question circled in her mind, and she shook her head, because there was no way she could make what she'd learned make sense. "Better just get organised," she said and began the task of laying out the supplies she'd need.

Matteo silently cursed the timing of James and his announcement, because it had the ability to undo things he'd barely begun to think may be within his grasp. He'd seen the shock on Constance's face, and seeing her response had hurt. Far more than it should have.

His friend stood by the communicase, waiting for him to take up the transmission receiver. "Hello?"

"Matteo? It's Felix. Your brother Javier has had an accident, and things are... It's not good here."

Felix was another life-long friend and possible half-brother—not that either side would or could acknowledge part-siblings in the environment of Casa Bonita.

"How? What's his status?" Matteo's hand clutched the receiver tightly.

"There was a scuffle in the bedroom, not a lot is known, because you know how secretive Javier has become. As to his status, I've heard he's in a bad way. The doors are closed, no one in and no one out. It's... It's bad, Matteo."

Matteo pictured the large white house, the columns, and heavy red doors on the front, while people milled around, waiting for the daily ration delivery. If the doors were closed...

"When did this happen?" He needed to know more.

"Yesterday. There was no ration delivery yesterday, so people went hungry. A day or two more and things will... You know, a civilisation on the edge of starvation is dangerous, and the food they hand out is barely enough now." Felix's voice took on a hushed quality. "I've heard too that something is coming. There's... People are scared." A sound echoed. "I have to go." The connection broke and Matteo stared at the communicase.

"Is there anyone else?"

James shock his head. "You know as well as I that the communicase devices were rounded up. It's only luck that Felix was able to find the parts and build his own."

It was true, the need had driven certain members to learn skills to ensure there was some kind of communication with the outside world.

"We need to get someone in there," Matteo said.

"I agree. But who? Most of our men are known to Javier, and any other male will need to be vetted. We need..." James' voice hushed. "We need a woman, I think. Someone willing to—"

"No," Matteo growled. "Not happening." He meant it too. He knew what the women had endured, and there was no way he'd ask any of them to take the chance.

"But Matteo, we need the information," James argued.

"Yes, we need information, but I'm not going to ask a woman to take the chances that would come with embedding in Casa Bonita."

"Then how will we get information?" James' eyes narrowed.

Matteo cocked his head. "We send fish. We pretend someone is selling fish to the house. We pick how and where we make contact, and if we play the cards right..."

James stared at him for a long moment. "That may work, but who...?"

Matteo scratched his head while he thought on the situation. "Who is working the boat at the moment?" he questioned, and James' eyes opened wide.

"Frank is. He's..."

"Young. In my employ. See if you can arrange a meeting, somewhere out of sight, and we might be able to gain some kind of insight." It wasn't going to be perfect, as Frank wasn't an insider, but he might be a suitable go-between for them and Felix. "With luck, we'll have Constance's suits by then."

James nodded. "I'll get onto it immediately. But if the suits aren't complete?"

Matteo shrugged. "We'll have to see what comes up then. Now, go. I'm going to see Constance about this first fitting, then I'll send you in."

He waited until James was out of sight. He hated the subversive nature of what he was doing, his preference would have been to be up-front, take his brother head-on, but that wasn't possible.

He inhaled once, then turned on his heel.

CONSTANCE HEARD Matteo enter the room and allowed herself a moment. Though she was drawn to him, she wasn't ready for anything to grow. She barely knew him, and that should be an indicator that nothing could occur.

"Are you ready for me, Constance?" Matteo's word choice jolted her; after all, she'd just been thinking something like that, hadn't she?

"Um, yes. Come, get on the dais, and I'll start taking your measurements." She tugged the tape from around her neck, where she'd slung it, and waited for him to step onto the half-barrel.

She took the length of his pants first and noted it down on the paper she'd stashed in her pocket, the pencil scrawling loudly in the quiet room. Even as she worked, she considered the stillness, the stiffness of his limbs.

"You need to loosen up, Matteo. Relax."

"I... I am loose." His mutter was muffled, as if he was holding onto the words with effort.

She stifled a laugh. "No, you're not. I can tell."

He shifted, and she continued her task.

"What?" he objected, startled as she moved to take his inside leg measurements.

"It's okay. I need to know how broad your legs are and the length of your inner leg." She could barely control her smile. "I've done this before—you can trust me."

"I... I do," he muttered, "but it's not..." he gulped, "It's not ladylike."

Constance rolled her eyes. "That's okay. I never said I was a lady. I'm a seamstress. My job is to make sure the suits fit properly, and I can't do that without taking all the measurements. Now stand still and let me finish my task."

She went back to her work. She knew most men didn't see her chosen job as appropriate for a young woman, but she was damned good at it. She took his chest and waist measurements. Then she moved to his back to take that as well.

Constance concentrated on finalising her measurements. "Hold out your arms," she muttered, and avoided his gaze, because for some weird reason, she didn't want to see the disappointment in his eyes as her hands moved swiftly.

"Constance." He moved and took her chin in his hand. "I'm sorry. I shouldn't have said..." He sighed.

"That's okay, Matteo. I know I'm not a lady, but now I'm done. Please send James in as soon as you're ready." She moved away to the table and wrote his name on the top of the paper and tucked it under the sewing machine base.

"Constance—"

"It's fine. Honestly. Now the sooner you send him in, the sooner I can begin the suits and begin on outfitting your men."

"Damn it," he growled. "Don't ignore me when I tell you I was wrong."

Her chest tightened. She wanted to believe him, but her inherent cynicism didn't allow her to ignore the truths she'd always known. She was little more than a 'mutt' of a house. An outcast who'd been born of a woman who'd had little value, and it was only because of her death that Constance's life changed. That single fact was why she'd been removed from the house environment.

Oh, she'd been well-educated and given every advantage, but it didn't change the truth. Nothing could.

The knowledge was a knife in her guts.

"Constance," his voice was just behind her.

She turned to find him there, standing mere inches away. "What, Matteo?" The cool demeanour she'd spent years polishing stood up to his appraisal, she was sure.

He raised a hand, cupped her cheek, and shock was a ricochet through her nervous system. "Don't turn away, please. I spoke unfairly. I didn't mean..."

"I know, Matteo. But I know who and what I am. Francesca was an anathema in a world that's patriarchal, and I accept that there will be the few who step out of the shadows, but not me. I'm not a leader or—" She swallowed.

"Rubbish," he said and dragged her head toward him. "You are an amazing woman. Beautiful, skilled, and I..." Confusion filled his gaze. "I want something I can't possibly ask of you," he whispered even as his lips touched hers.

The touch was... It was like wildfire rushing through her entire body, the spark beginning at her mouth and spreading with the speed of a net electric charge. Her hands clutched at him, found the lapels of his jacket, and held tight as her senses whirled.

When he tugged away, she was adrift. Bereft. She didn't know why, but when he ended the contact, all she knew was that he'd withdrawn the contact that was deep and strangely fulfilling.

"I'm sorry, Constance. That was unwarranted, and I... My apologies."

She flinched. "Fine. I will forget this occurred," she muttered and turned away as the burn of tears made itself known. I won't cry. Blinking furiously, she muttered, "I need to see James now."

He moved. She heard him, felt him draw near, but she remained determinedly looking at her table, and he moved away. She heard him stamp to the door, and when it finally thudded, she exhaled.

"Stupid," she muttered. "Why would he want someone like you?" Now she dashed at the moisture that dampened her cheeks.

What the hell were you thinking? The refrain wound through him. He'd seen the fragile tension which surrounded her before he'd left the room in the hunching of her shoulders, but Matteo wasn't sure he knew how to undo the damage he'd done.

He was stomping off when James came into view. "You need to go…" he all but growled, and when James frowned at him, he knew he'd need to explain. "See if Constance is all right. I said some things…" Not for one moment would he admit what he'd done.

He scrubbed a hand through his hair as James nodded and headed for the room.

I need to get my head right. He stepped out of the building and glanced around, noting steady stream of movement coming and going. His protocols had clearly been put in place as women trundled into the compound and men were busy erecting the canvas tents which would house them and the children.

The main house had been opened, windows and doors, while women were out in the gardens harvesting.

They knew what was at stake and had begun the process of preparing to stay safe while he was lost in his recriminations.

"I have a job to do," he snarled and moved toward the gates.

Chapter Ten

AFTER JAMES LEFT THE ROOM, Constance settled down to begin redrafting the pattern. Her hands moved with sure and quick ease, pencil scratching over paper as she marked it up, writing names on it as she worked.

No one entered her work zone, and when she realised the light was dimming, she rose and turned on the electric lights and returned to her task, unrolling the first heavy material to pin and cut.

She'd barely begun to slice through the material when three knocks interrupted. She raised her head. "Yes?"

A young girl entered the room. "Matteo and James have asked if you'll join them for dinner."

Her stomach rumbled and she realised just how many hours had passed. "Oh. Yes," she answered. It wasn't that she wanted to see him, but she'd need to eat. "Should I come...?"

"Yes, now, miss. They're in his dining room, so if you'd follow me?"

She rose, dusting off her hands as she followed the young woman through the hall.

The scent of chicken teased her senses, and once more her stomach gurgled, giving away just how hungry she now knew she'd become.

As she entered the dining area, she noted that only Matteo stood there.

"Excuse me, miss, I need to do some things in the kitchen," the girl said and then left the room so there was just the two of them there.

"James is seeing to some details, but he'll join us for dinner in a few minutes." He appeared ill at ease, shifting from one foot to the other. "I am sorry about this afternoon."

She felt the same pressure building inside her. "There's no—"

"There is," he pressed. "I don't regret kissing you, but I do apologise for forcing myself upon you. I..." He shrugged.

A chink of something, a whisper of a lighter emotion, took root in her chest. "Matteo?" She swallowed, because she was about to bare her soul in a way she'd never done before, because the urgency told her that she needed to. That this moment may be a one-off, but she wasn't going to make him suffer. "I... I don't regret it either."

He rocked back, his gaze searching hers. "You don't?"

She shook her head. "I know life is fleeting. That humans are weak, and we must take chances offered. I understand that."

God knew, after Amaryllis had been injured and Francesca abducted, she did! The death of her mother was simply one more time when life had played her for a fool.

"I enjoyed it," he whispered and smiled.

Her eyes popped wider open. How do you respond to that? "Ah, Matteo, we should sit down and wait for the meal," she answered, because nothing came to mind.

Three years in London hadn't taught her how to deal with such comments, nor did anything that had come before. Oh, young men had made overtures, but nothing so overt. The confusion had her glancing away so he wouldn't see her reaction.

"Wait," Matteo called.

She looked up at him with surprise. "What?"

He crowded in close, a glint of something in his eyes. "Let me say, it was a pleasure," and his voice dropped into a deeper and far more intimate band.

Her breath fled.

He took her hand and dragged her up against his chest, and he kissed her again.

This time, while she was still unprepared for the emotions that stirred inside her, she was ready for his touch, curling her hands over his shoulders while the energy zinged through her body.

His lips were firm, demanding more from her, and she responded, opening her mouth slightly, enough to taste the whisper of him, the dark heat invading her body, and when he pulled away, she stared at him. "What was…?"

"I don't know why I feel this need, Constance, but I do." He stepped away and tugged at his shirt collar, and she felt an inexplicable desire to wind her arms around his waist.

Does he realise he gave himself away? That he's not as unmoved as he thinks he is?

"And you're right. We should sit down." He led the way to the table, pulled out a chair, and waited for her to seat herself.

Her brain worked sluggishly, and it wasn't until he was opposite her that she was able to wash away the cobwebs in her brain. "I've started cutting the material for your suit. I should be able to begin pinning it tonight, then I'll tack it together."

"Tack it?" he queried.

"It's a kind of stitch used to hold the material in place, so it doesn't move during the sewing. Sometime tomorrow morning I should be able to do the first fitting, pinned of course, to make sure I've got all the cuts right."

"I don't remember doing that with a suit maker." He rubbed a hand over his chin, and she felt the somersault of her stomach in reaction.

Did he realise that drew her eyes to his face? His lips? She controlled her reaction, schooled her features to remain impassive. "No, they tend to sew a little differently, things like jacket arms are structured fittings, with chalking and pins, but this isn't the same. There's no lining, and this material is meant to fit like a glove."

"I see." He shook his head. "And you have…"

"Oh, I spent time learning that while in London too. I believe that knowing as much as possible allows you to be better at what you do." She nodded just as James entered the room.

"Better at what?" James enquired.

"Sewing," she answered while Matteo replied, "everything she does."

The burn of a blush scorched her skin.

James looked from her to Matteo and shook his head. "I have a feeling there is more to the conversation than you're telling me." He settled himself at the table between them. "I've made the arrangements you've requested, Matteo. The compound will enter lockdown when we leave, and I've found guards..."

"Guards? Lockdown? What's happening, Matteo?" Constance asked.

"My brother had an accident, as you know, and it's possibly the chance to do something about saving Casa Bonita's inhabitants."

"How dangerous is that?" Constance asked.

"It's likely going to be very dangerous. It's why I want the suits for my people," Matteo said.

"You'll be going with your men?" Constance worried her lip.

"I wouldn't ask them to go into a situation I wouldn't be prepared to face." The meal was delivered to the table, and apart from a brief "thanks" to the girl serving, he waited quietly until the room only held the three of them again. "I have a responsibility to my men and those who are stuck in Casa Bonita, Constance. Anything less is cowardice. But this trip is a chance to find out more, not to attack."

She considered his words and didn't like the way she felt, realising he'd be facing danger. "When Haven House was destroyed, my father and Amaryllis both were in the thick of things. That's how Ammy lost her leg."

James passed the plate of chicken and vegetables to her, and she took a moment, considering and choosing before pushing it back.

"Then Francesca was looking after the injured when she was abducted after the fall of Nobel Crest," Constance continued.

"You're not going with me," boomed Matteo. "That would be ridiculous."

James watched them; she saw the way his gaze moved between them as they spoke, but she couldn't seem to control her tongue. "I'm not asking to. I don't have anything or any gifts that would assist. I'll stay here and keep producing suits but..."

"There's no but, Constance. You will remain here, safe. The compound is guarded and—"

She rose. "Look, I'm not some silly debutante. I know here is the right place for me. I was just going to say that you should take Father's pantheras with you. I can show you how to control them. And you'd have known that if you just let me speak!" The pulse in her throat jumped and quivered, and her grip on her knife and fork were deathly, knuckles white. "What did you think I was going to do? Say I'd fight? I can't hit the side of a barn with an actinic gun, let alone a normal one!"

"I... Forgive me, Constance. I was..." He sighed. "We should eat." His gaze dropped, and Constance realised they'd just given James quite a show, and her blush returned, heating her face.

"Forgive me, James. Matteo. I suddenly don't feel hungry." She started to push away from the table.

"Don't... Don't go, Constance. Stay," Matteo said. "Eat. I promise I'll attempt to be more temperate in my decorum."

His words were so urbane, and yet, when she glanced at him, shame had painted his face red, and she took pity on him. She'd never been easy to live with, and while they'd barely spent two days in the same location, it appeared her flawed character, her desire to argue, had once again struck. *I really need to learn to control my tongue and myself.*

"I... All right then," she answered and sank back into her chair.

The rest of the meal continued in silence.

Constance had eaten and excused herself, retiring to her bedroom, when James turned to his friend and drawled, "You were a bit quick off the mark there, Matteo."

Matteo felt his lips turn into a grimace. "I just... I don't know what got into me. She's... I don't know."

"Really? I mean I've watched the way you watch her. You want something, and I'm pretty sure it's more than a simple roll in the hay, isn't it?" James' words hit a nerve.

"As if a woman like that would accept a man like me," he growled, stung by the words of his closest friend.

"*Why?*" James pointed to her closed bedroom door. "Tell me what you don't have that a woman like that would want? You're smart. Look at what you've amassed from an extremely small stake."

"I had good advisors," Matteo answered.

"Yes, but you also had the good sense to listen to them. Damn it. Yes, you're the second son, and you've had to make yourself, but you've done more for others than most would. The money you've made has allowed you to create a safe place for these people. You've taken in, housed, fed, and clothed them. You've given their children a safe future, where they will be giving back to society. You've given them hope. A woman like that? She sees the value, because she's been there too. You know that."

Matteo didn't want to hear that, because somehow it made the hope inside him grow. "Stop it, James."

"No, Matteo. You need to hear it. You've done remarkable things, and if she's not able to see—"

"I didn't give her a chance though." His shoulders slumped. "Yes, I do want..." He sighed and looked heavenward. "What if she wants more? What if I fail?"

James shook his head, sorrow in his gaze. "*We all fail at some point. Sometimes the things we fail at are the things that matter the most, but we must keep trying. We all aren't always right, nor are we always wrong. But if you don't take the chance, you'll never know. Don't let regrets eat away at you.*"

Suddenly Matteo understood what the man before him was saying. James had been betrothed to a beautiful and vivacious lady, until the woman he'd loved had been taken to the house and married to Javier. Yet another wife to be used and abused and little more than a number, and all James could do was watch. It had torn him apart, and he'd been ejected from the house after one too many outbursts of fury against both Javier and the system of Casa Bonita.

James had grieved that loss for a long time, and only recently had he understood he couldn't have stopped what happened, and Matteo had stood beside him the entire time.

"I'm sorry, James. I didn't..."

"I know, but that's why I also know you can't wait. If you want her, you're going to have to move quickly. Life isn't fair or easy, but if she reciprocates your feelings, then you should act on them." James inhaled a shuddering breath. "I'm going to retire. I'll see you in the morning." He left the room, and Matteo watched him go and considered the words James had flung at him.

Constance perched on the side of the bed, feeling foolish. The argument she'd begun had been unnecessary. Just another in a long line of them. She'd heard the raised voices from the lounge, the thud of a door, and deduced James had left to go wherever he slept. Another thud had likely been Matteo.

Exhaustion and frustration ate at her. At home, she'd have risen and gone to her sewing and worked out what bothered her. But here...? The emotional turmoil within her wouldn't allow her to rest, she knew from experience. Constance didn't want to wander around the building; after all, what if he was awake? Found her? She sighed again, because what else was there for her to do, since sleep was a long way from a reality? She rose.

"I'll just go get what is ready to work on and bring it back here." She'd get a good start on her work. She'd work until she could sleep, and maybe it would soothe her ragged nerves.

There was a straight-backed chair in the corner, it would see her right, and the lamp on the chest of drawers would give her adequate light, as she wasn't doing the intricate stitches of a gown.

Constance opened the door a little way and peered into the room. It felt furtive as she made her way quickly across the room, the swish of her gown the only sound. The door to the hallway beckoned, and she cracked it enough to push through then closed it with careful moves.

She dashed down the hallway and reached for the door. Pushing it open, she came to a stop.

There was Matteo, his shirt removed as he stretched before a large, round sack.

His back was lined with scars. Long and ridged. She inhaled, and the sound must have alerted him to her presence as he turned toward her.

"Constance," he muttered. "I thought you'd retired."

Her fingers fluttered to her lips. "Your back," she whispered.

He reached for his shirt and started to tug it on, and she called, "Wait!"

She stepped up to him, behind him, and touched a light finger to one of the longer and deeper scars.

"What happened?" she asked softly.

"I tried to free a woman," he muttered. "My brother ensured I'd never forget I was less than him. Unworthy." Fury scoured his response.

"I'm so sorry that happened to you." She rose up and laid her lips upon the scar, wanting nothing more than to take away the pain these marks clearly still inflicted on him.

"Constance, don't," he growled.

Tears formed and she slid her fingers along the marred plane of his back. "Why? These are marks of honour, Matteo. If you tried to save her—"

"I failed." Tension radiated from him.

"You tried, Matteo. That's more than most would do. It doesn't make you unworthy or less. It makes you more." She meant those words and needed him to hear them. She rounded him and took his hands. "See me. See that what I'm telling you is honest, Matteo. There is no lack of honour if you truly did what was right, immaterial of the outcome." She cupped his cheek. "You paid a very high price. Did you love her?" She held in her breath, waiting for his answer.

"She was my sister. She was only sixteen when they took her away, and I'd have done anything for her, but now she's... *Nadia's* beyond my help. She died giving birth, and that's when I finally understood that this had to end. When James lost his betrothed, he followed me, and we planned..." He closed his eyes, and she felt the pain he tried to hide.

"That's when you purchased this land. Built the compound," she finished.

He nodded and opened his eyes. "I wanted to build a safe place."

Emotions swirled around them: sadness, impotence, and more. A hunger began to build inside her.

"Matteo, you're a good man."

He laughed, the sound discordant. "No, I'm not. I'm trying to be better but—"

She stopped him the only way she knew how, kissing him.

Her lips on his, and this time, she opened to him first. Felt him tense, then his hands wrapped around her, and she felt every inch of his body melding against hers, the bite of his fingers at her waist as he held her close, and her body... She moved, just a tiny slide, but nerve endings sang at the beauty of their forms pressed tightly together.

His mouth left hers, and it roamed over her jaw, and she reacted, mindless with a hunger she'd never felt before. The emptiness in the pit of her stomach and the sharp pleasure grew as her breasts slid over his body.

"Constance, we can't..." he muttered but kept moving, his lips sliding over the skin of her neck, and she arched up, wanting more.

"Oh, Matteo, what you make me feel," she muttered, then staggered when he let her go.

"We can't... Constance, I..."

Her hand rose to her breast. It was beating so fast she feared it would burst from her chest. "What are you doing to me, Matteo? You make me feel things, and I... I don't want to stop," she said, her confusion clear in the threadiness of her voice.

His eyes glittered in the low light. "Constance, I want you. You can feel that."

Her breath caught. "But?"

"I am not able to give you what you want. I'm dedicated to the total destruction of Casa Bonita. I'm not a choice you want to make." He spoke with a firmness she hadn't heard from him before.

Fury filled her. "How do you know what I want?" *How dare he make my decisions for me?*

"Your body is betraying you, Constance. I see the rosy colour of your skin. I see the way your nerves are jumping. You're too innocent—"

She laughed, the sound bitter, and she backed away from him. "Oh yeah, I'm so innocent that I don't know what intimacy is." She turned to the table and started to gather up the material, her moves jerky. "I know what I want. It was you, but now? You can take your—"

"Constance, please. Listen to me…" He placed a hand on her shoulders, but she tugged away. She wanted his touch but jerked hard against him, knowing that only space would allow her to think sensibly.

"Leave me alone, Matteo. Go do your hero thing, and leave me be." She hurried for the door, her hands full of material. All she wanted was to escape this room and the desire which still coursed through her veins.

Outside the door, tears burst free, trickling down her cheeks, but she ignored them and scurried up the hall. She didn't want to stay here, not under these circumstances, yet she had a job to do.

Tomorrow she'd contact her father and… *And what? So, Constance, are you planning on telling him everything? That Matteo kissed you and you kissed him? That he makes you feel things that you don't want to label?*

Once in the bedroom, she dumped all the material onto the bed then slumped down beside it. "What am I supposed to do?" she wailed.

Settling once more, wiping the tears from her face, she looked out the window, noting the dim glow of the township beyond the compound. Others were in worse straits. They had no future. They had no education and children who needed to be housed, fed, dressed.

Even in her disappointment, she could still find enjoyment. She would, damn it! Damien and Amaryllis had given her a future and hope, and giving up wasn't an option. It was up to her what she did with those opportunities and to share the rewards of her luck.

Wallowing for a long time had never been her way, and she wouldn't allow this to stop her from achieving… something. She had choices. She had the funds.

A seed of a plan began to emerge as she scrubbed her face. "Go to bed, Constance. When you wake in the morning, you can begin the process of making a difference."

Chapter Eleven

HE'D HURT Constance and that scoured Matteo. But he couldn't commit to anything bar the task he'd set himself when he'd left Casa Bonita. So, he settled in his office, looking over the information he'd already gleaned.

James had already planned how he would talk to the fisherman who was working Matteo's business. But, as always, that would take time. James would need to travel, and he'd already sent a message to Damien, given his super-quick dirigible was still at the port. But then James would need to find out where Felix would be, so he could make a bargain with the man. Meanwhile, Constance would continue to create the safety suits from the ballistafabric she'd brought with her.

He scratched the notes on the pad in front of him, and scrubbed his face as he made a list of the unknown facts.

How many would be present on the island was a significant fact that was currently unknown. The range of skills were issues as well. Had they fortified further on top of the electrified fencing and actinic projectiles from the parapets?

He closed his eyes to visualise the building and layout and didn't realise just how tired he was. When he opened his eyes, it was morning, the light of sunrise glinting in through the windows.

"What...?" Shoving from the table, he grunted and looked around.

He headed up the hall to the bedroom and was surprised to see Constance's bedroom door was open. He stepped toward it.

"Constance?"

Silence.

He moved toward the bedroom. "Constance?" He spun and looked around the small house, and noted the front door lay open, and a lump took up residence in his chest. "Constance? Where are you?"

Stepping into the courtyard, he pulled up short, noticing the auto that he'd driven the day before, heading out the gates.

"Damn it!" He thrust his hands deep into his pants pockets.

"She's got her guard with her, but I'm sure she won't be long," James said from behind him.

"What? She's not... gone?" He turned and stared at James.

"Why would she? Did you say something to her?" James queried, and Matteo wanted to say no. He wished that was the truth.

"I... I think I... Damn it, I did and said inexcusable things. Some without thinking, and some was purely an accident." He tugged his hands through his hair.

"Huh. You're usually the one who knows the right way to say things, and who smooths over everyone else's issues." James laughed. "Come on. Let's go eat. She'll probably be back before you're finished."

If only it were that simple. His heart and his gut ached at the realisation that he may have made the worst decision of his life.

❧

"Miss Constance, should we be doing this? I believe Mr Bonita is in the process of planning an incursion to Casa Bonita. If the word gets out..." Anderton frowned. "Perhaps you could have used Mr Bonita's personal communicase?"

She shook her head. "No. I need to talk with my father about my plans, as well as other personal issues, and Mr Bonita's unit is in his parlour, so privacy would be an issue. Also, I left some items behind on the Phoenix, which I need to retrieve." She didn't quite have the heart to tell him exactly what she was thinking. A long night of soul-searching and consideration had brought her to this point, but nothing could occur without her father's assistance.

The early morning light filled her with the hope that had been missing during the dark hours, and as she pulled up the vehicle to the dock, she knew she'd made the right decision. Climbing from the automotive, she headed up the stairs to the long wooden area, and via the gangplank, she boarded the Phoenix.

"Miss Constance!" The captain hurried forth. "Are you... Are we taking you home with us this morning?" His eyes were half-closed and surprise coloured his words.

"No, Captain. I need to use the communicase and wish you to remain docked until my father gives further directions." She swept past him and headed for the communication system in the parlour.

She sent an initial text communication to the base system, which she knew from experience was manned all day, every day by a member of the household.

<Need to have discussion with Master. Urgent. Reply with time. Constance>

She kept it short so it would convey the urgency of her request. When would he reply? She knew he had no planned travels, and he tended to rise early to achieve the paperwork before heading to the manufactory to oversee the day's progress.

The machine chattered and spat out a message.

<Contact now. Damien>

With shaking hands, Constance lifted the receiver and sent the ping that would allow the machines to make contact.

"Constance?" Damien's voice came over the line.

"Father? I've made a decision. I am going to stay here. I..." How to tell him the next bit? "I wish to purchase a property and set up my business here."

For a moment, silence filled the air. "Why?" he finally asked.

"There's a need. The women have little or no paid work, and I see that as a need I can fill. The fabric can be shipped here. It will make no real difference where I am, so long as there are no hiccups in the supply line. I will need to find a property which can be suitably guarded. There are men here to fill the security gap. They've come from houses, so they understand what's at stake, and they need employment. The region has little funds. I can... We can make a difference, Father. But I need access to my trust to make this happen."

Once again, the silence came close to unnerving her. "All right, but as per the terms of our agreement, I will need to come and check the arrangements before any contract is signed or monies paid."

The money had been transferred into an account in her name once Amaryllis and Damien had officially adopted her. He'd done the same for all his children, and not for the first time was Constance thankful for the kindnesses she and her siblings had experienced. She also knew Damien felt his responsibilities keenly, hence the reason he'd want to check to ensure that she'd chosen a safe and secure location and would likely want to know why she'd made such a decision. And he'd want to do it sooner rather than later.

"Have you found a suitable location?" he queried.

"No. I plan to make enquiries today. There's more than a few empty buildings and houses too, from what I noticed on arrival yesterday." She glanced to the doorway as Anderton entered carrying a cup of tea, and she smiled at him, to thank the man for his kindness.

"I'll be there in a few days. Meanwhile, keep Anderton close. And Constance?"

"Yes, Father?" She blinked, knowing Damien rarely asked much in return.

"Stay on the compound and safe. I've heard there's rumblings of unrest at Casa Bonita, and when that's the case, house masters usually send men looking for scapegoats, no matter how far afield. I'll give direction for the Phoenix to remain there until I'm satisfied that all the necessary services and security are in place. The men can be co-opted to provide extra security until such time as I'm happy with the set-up at your location." There was a thread of uneasiness in his voice. One she couldn't remember hearing in a long time. Not since Francesca—

"Yes, Father. Thank you, and I will follow your directions."

They concluded the call, and she sat back to consider what her father had told her. He'd heard rumblings, and that was what Matteo had heard too. Even so, it wouldn't cease her planning. Matteo might not want her, but she'd finally—hopefully, anyway—found the answer to the conundrum of how to be useful in her future, a problem she'd been toying with for years.

She'd told the truth when she'd explained that she loved what she did, but there was more. She wanted to make a difference, no matter how small. If the women she'd seen with the children could be empowered to make a life, take on a role that would pay them a wage. To assist their children in building a future? Then her life would have been worthwhile.

"Anderton? I want to see the town. I think... I'm planning to stay here if I can find a suitable property or two."

His eyes widened. "And the master?"

She nodded, understanding what he was asking. "I can't sign any contracts until he agrees, but we can find the location of my home and workshop. If they're within an easy distance, that would be acceptable. So, let us eat, then we'll go look around the town. Who knows? You might like it enough to remain too."

He smiled and she patted his hand before he left the room.

She rose and brushed off her skirt, feeling that finally, she was making the decisions around how she'd lead her life from this point on.

<h1 style="text-align:center">Chapter Twelve</h1>

MATTEO SNARLED and stalked as the hours passed.

James entered the room. "Still nothing?" he asked.

"She's been seen in town, walking around, looking in buildings. Apart from that, I have no idea what the hell she's playing at."

Matteo shoved his fists into his pockets as he looked out the window. In his experience, women didn't leave the men in the dark. They sought assistance, they... Matteo shook his head, because that knowledge was coloured by his experience of the houses, and Constance didn't adhere to any of the behaviours that were house-bound.

No house would have allowed her to travel to London to hone her craft.

No master would have sent her here, with a man she wasn't married to, and let her manage her time.

The reality was, if her movements were regulated by a house, she'd be little more than a chattel.

James seemed to understand the arguments running through his friend's head, and he simply shook his head and left Matteo to stew in his discontent.

Matteo's mind jumped around, trying to work out what she was up to. The township of Bald Head wasn't large. The infrastructure was only just now starting to catch up with the swelling numbers who were relocating because of the compound.

"If only I could do more," Matteo muttered.

Yes, he was housing them and giving them safety, and small businesses were popping up around the town. A stable, a market garden, and even a small weekly market where farmers could sell their produce. The school was growing, and buildings seemed to be erected almost daily now.

A sound broke through his introspection, and he looked out the window to see the automotive entering the compound. When it stopped outside the building he stomped to the door, meaning to swing it open and demand answers.

Before he had time to open the door, James was at the automotive, assisting Constance to alight and speaking animatedly, hands flying. Matteo took the moment to rein in his temper and watched the byplay until Anderton, Constance's guard, moved beside her. Matteo's hand grasped the knob, tore open the door, and he stalked toward the small knot.

"What the hell do you think you were doing?" he growled.

Constance turned slowly, an impassive expression on her face. "I was undertaking some forward planning. I don't answer to you, and my father is fully apprised of the situation. He will be here in a day or so to complete my work in town. Until then, I have tasks to complete in the office. Now, if you'll excuse me."

He watched as she flounced off, the hem of her skirt swaying in time with her footsteps. Matteo made to follow her, but James stilled him with a hand on his chest.

"Leave her for now. Anderton, come with us," his friend demanded and headed back to where Matteo had waited.

They gathered around the table, and Matteo took a moment to inhale, so he wouldn't be too loud asking the question which roasted him from within his guts.

"What's going on?" His demand was growled, and the two men exchanged glances.

"I suppose we're not going to like it," answered James. "Anderton?"

"She's looking to purchase property. To live in. To build a business."

The man kept his answer terse, his face stern, then he shrugged. "Whatever happened to her yesterday and last night, she's decided, and sought assistance from Damien Whitmore. He's due to arrive tomorrow or the day after to ensure the building she's chosen is safe, and he's bringing a small number of guards to begin the process of protecting her and her investment."

Matteo couldn't say what surprised him the most. That she'd planned so much in a short time, or the depths of what she'd already done without even taking the time to talk to him! *And why would she? You made it clear to her that nothing can eventuate.*

"Which. Building?"

Anderton cleared his throat. "The one that was apparently built for the mercantile which never opened and the residence above it. There's ample space for her to work and to train staff."

"Train staff?" Matteo thought he sounded like a parrot.

"Yes. Women who want to learn to sew. Women to sell the products she's planning to make, and others to handle the mail-order side," Anderton explained.

Matteo blinked. "Mail-order?"

James cleared his throat. "Many women who are unable to get to locations will purchase their clothing and that of their children, particularly if they don't sew themselves, from mail-order. Others purchase fabrics and threads and..." He cleared his throat. "Whatever they need to make their own clothes."

"But what about the ballistafabric suits?" He hated that he was focussed on them more than her needs and desires, but he had responsibilities. A plan.

"I believe she has plans for that too. It's a large building, and when she walked through it, she was surprised by the size of the main area, prospective fitting rooms, and she talked about a more secured area toward the back."

Matteo grunted at Anderton's reply and turned around to glance out the window. "I'm not sure that's a great idea. Maybe after—"

"I make my own decisions, Matteo."

He whirled and noted that Constance now stood in the doorway, her hat removed and her hair tied back in an intricate knot. Her face was pale, but he read a determination in the tight muscles of her face and neck.

"Thank you, Anderton and James, but if I could talk to Matteo alone?"

She stepped aside to allow the two men to leave the room, and Matteo marshalled his thoughts. "Why would you want to leave?"

Her eyes glinted. "Really? You can't work it out? I didn't take you for..." She waved a hand. "I won't stay here, Matteo, because you don't seem capable of realising that I can and am more than able to decide what I want."

"But the suits..."

She rolled her eyes. "As Anderton explained, there is an area I can secure at the back of the building, so your precious suits can be made. My father is due to arrive hopefully tomorrow, which means that within the week, I should be able to move in."

He opened and closed his mouth, but what was there to say?

"So, until then, I'll focus on your suit and James' then begin taking measurements for your men. Now, if you'll excuse me, I'll get to work. I'll need the office space, as I finished tacking your suit last night."

He watched as she swept from the room. "God damn it all!" he roared and kicked the chair beside him.

Constance huddled before the sewing machine, feeling the movement of the needle as it swept up and down through the material. It was slow going, but the specially reinforced thread was keeping an easy pace as it slid through the fabric.

Her hands smoothed over the stitches, checking the tension and ensuring the material remained undamaged. The pants lay on the chair beside her, after a marathon three-hour session. The weight of the material and the nature of the thread made stitching almost laborious. She knew it was probably long past time to retire, but if she could just finish this one side...

She yawned and looked up.

Matteo's gaze met hers. "You should get some sleep," he said with a frown.

"I'll go soon, thank you. But you might as well retire. I just need to finish this section." She reached for the cup of water that she kept beside her in such circumstances and sipped again, needing the refreshment to keep her alert just a little longer.

"I'll stay until you do," he muttered, and she shrugged.

"Your choice, I guess," she said and returned to the task.

Her brain wanted to prosecute the argument that she fought to ignore, but she held her tongue. After all, that would be far too revealing. Instead, she allowed her mind to drift once more. Her head nodding...

Matteo had known the instant she'd fallen asleep, and he rose, carefully slid her hands from the machine, and he switched it off at the wall. Constance's subtle scent teased him, as did a stray lock of hair, as he moved her to the settee he'd had brought in when he realised, she wasn't going to stop anytime soon. He'd told himself he'd wait for her, and he'd watched, but she'd worked right up to the evening meal, and he'd had to urge her to stop and eat. She'd returned to the machine, and he'd watched again, all the while pretending he was checking the figures in his log.

He moved to open the door then returned to lift her against his chest, taking great pains not to wake her. She'd worked herself to a state of exhaustion, and he wondered just how many times she had done that in the past.

Stepping carefully, he carried the bundle in his arms down the corridor to the living area and laid her on the lounge. He moved into the bedroom and collected pillows and a blanket.

She only stirred long enough to whisper, "Where...?" before her eyes closed again.

He settled himself in the armchair and watched as she slept. Her face pale, her hair a halo that spread around her head. He'd nearly dozed off when her sleep turned restless.

"Noooo…" she murmured and twisted on the narrow seat. "Don't… Don't want to remember," she breathed, and he frowned, leaned in.

"It's all right, Constance. You're safe." His hand itched to touch her hair, to soothe her, but he shoved it deep into a pocket.

"Hide," she whispered.

Every word she muttered tore him up. *What had she hidden from? Who?* "What are your secrets, Constance? What don't you want anyone to know?"

She didn't answer, having fallen back into a quieter phase of rest, and he moved back to his chair, determined he'd find out, and if possible, assist her.

Chapter Thirteen

WHEN CONSTANCE WOKE, she lay on the sofa, and she tried to piece together how she'd come to be here. Her back ached abominably, but not as much as she'd found in the past. More than once she'd dozed off while working on a project.

The room was shrouded in darkness, and long seconds passed before she spied feet, legs... trousers. Matteo.

He dozed in the armchair opposite, and she sighed.

Why did he do such caring things on one hand then on the other refuse to give any credibility to the attraction she knew they both felt?

The kisses... Well, they weren't her first, but they were the only ones that demanded more than a brief caress. They'd driven her to forget propriety.

Even now, the feel of him echoed in her mind, and she laid her fingers against her lips.

"I won't settle for less," she said quietly.

"Nor should you," Matteo answered, and she startled.

"You're supposed to be asleep," she muttered, and he laughed.

"I'm a light sleeper. Too many years at Casa Bonita not to. But I... You must understand, I have a commitment, Constance. One I take seriously. There are too many there who need my help."

She nodded. "I know, but you don't have to ignore one to do the other, Matteo. I... I want something more than a long life without passion." The words were spoken slowly, with intention, because she needed him to understand. "With you, I feel."

He sighed and tipped back his head, fingers pinching the bridge of his nose. "Constance, I want you. I want to know you, to be with you, but I can't promise that. Not now, and until I can, I'm not willing to—"

"I'm not asking you to marry me," she said as she stood up, feeling the flash of ire. She turned around, needing a moment to clear her head, to think how to explain what she did want. "Look, I'm not one to make foolish choices or to rush anything. Or at least not usually. But I'm leaving here within the week, because I finally chose what I wanted. Not what someone thought I should do. I see what you're doing, the way you're giving others a chance to build a life, and I want to make a difference too."

She twined her fingers as she considered how to explain the need that she'd banked for years. The yearning to be more that she'd had to ignore until the opportunity rose.

"I can do that by teaching other women to sew, by employing them and giving them a future. Until now I didn't know how to give something to others." Constance shook her head, trying to clear the emotion that clouded her ability to explain. "I couldn't adopt a child like Damien and Amaryllis. I'm not a physiotraducere like Francesca, who can repair broken bodies, or run a house like Raphael. My brothers and sisters, they're equally talented or skilled. They give back daily. Everyone except me has a path, Matteo."

Her chest bellowed, and hot tears stung.

"For years, I've wanted to be different. I want to do something useful." She flung out her hand. "Yes, I can make these damned ballistafabric suits, but they're still not new or even life-changing ..."

He laughed, and she drew back. "Not life-changing? I saw Damien shoot you. Thought you were dead until you stood up. You'll give us a chance to—"

"No, I don't. I sew it, but I didn't invent the fabric. That was my friend and her father, and they're amazing, but I don't fool myself thinking I'm more. I simply make the best of what they have. Of my skills. But now I see how I can help, and I'm going to, Matteo. When Ammy and Damien took us on, he settled a trust on each of us, to give us the chance when we knew how to do good. This is my way. My path. This is how I'll make a difference."

Can't he see that? Doesn't he understand that I need to leave a legacy of good? Something to outweigh the darkness I've dragged through my life.

He shot up, stalked over, and grabbed her shoulders, the grip hard and biting, but she welcomed it, the strength of him. "You're enough, Constance."

"No, I'm not." The words were nearly a scream, and she tried to tug away, but he held her tight, looked and waited until she returned his burning gaze. "I need to know that whatever I am, whatever I do, I'll matter. This is what matters and..." She swiped at the tears on her cheeks. "I'm crying more than I ever have. It's your fault," she muttered thickly.

This time when he laughed it didn't sting. "I have a habit of doing that to those who matter. Constance, I wish I could offer you myself." His voice deepened. "I wish I could offer you forever." His gaze roamed over her. "I can only offer you now."

"I'll take it, Matteo." And she sealed it by reaching up to his lips and kissing him.

Heat exploded in Matteo's belly, and he gripped her tight, feeling the softness of her body against his own.

He groaned and tugged away. "Be sure, Constance. Once we do this, there's no going back."

Her eyes glittered in the lamplight. "I don't want to go back, Matteo. I know what I'm doing." He gave her another moment and her lips pursed. "Please."

The word was his undoing. As his lips settled on hers again, his hands circled her tiny waist, and he dragged her closer. The kiss was scorching as their mouths tangled. Her hair seemed to fall from the confines of her knot, and he twined a strand around a finger and tugged just enough that her head fell back, exposing the long line of her neck, the beating pulse that jumped.

"God, Constance, you're beautiful," he muttered, and his lips found that spot, tongue flicking over the vein, and she gasped.

"Matteo? Please!"

His fingers discovered the fasteners of her gown hidden against her spine, and they tugged and pulled, needing to release her from the confines of the material that hid the miles of skin he knew lay beneath, as his body demanded more, with an urgency he'd never experienced. "Damn it," he growled, and she chuckled.

"Want help?" She spoke with a throaty rasp that sent shocks of lightning direct to his groin.

"I want you out of this thing," he stated, and she laughed.

"Let me then." She stepped away, and their gazes meshed as her hands moved to her back, working with a sureness that told him she regularly dressed without assistance.

The bodice of her gown loosened, and he hissed a breath.

"You can do the rest, if you'd like," Constance offered, and he took her shoulders, turned her gently. Undid the button at the back of her neck.

"There's a buckle at the side. Each side," she informed him, and he growled again.

"Damn fool new-fangled clothing ideas." His fingers worked at the clasp. "Who thought these were a good idea?"

She chuckled. "Me. I designed these clothes and manufactured them. The London ladies adore them."

"They can keep them. For now, they're a pain in my rear," he whispered against her ear, and she shivered.

Constance shrugged the bodice off and stepped back so it fell to the floor. "Well now, I didn't design it for this reason, but it's very convenient." She smiled at him, and his eyes glowed in the dim light.

"Yes. Certainly, very convenient, but not high on my list of interest just now." He swooped in, pulling her against him, his lips finding her sensitive jawline as she shivered and allowed her hands to rest against his chest. She felt the heat of him, and the power.

Her hands curled up and over his shoulders as she arched, granting him access once again to the line of her neck. "Matteo," she muttered.

His hands worked at the fastener of her skirt, and finally, it too dropped away with a gentle thud. "So beautiful," he growled, kissing the skin of her shoulder, before bending down and lifting her into his arms.

"What…?"

"The bedroom. This is going to be better for you there." He opened the door, carried her into his room, and shut the world out with a well-placed kick before sliding her down to the soft surface.

It took a few seconds before her sight adjusted to the dimness of the unlit room, and she spied him, removing his shirt, and she licked her lips. She wanted him, knew the mechanics of the act, but the heat which coiled low in her belly was new, and something she associated with only him.

"Constance?" He was watching her now.

"Matteo?" She raised an eyebrow. "Second thoughts?"

He sputtered with laughter. "It's supposed to be me saying that, giving you the chance to stop this before it goes too far."

"No. I want this, and you. Matteo, please come and make love to me." For the first time, she needed someone to be with her. To love her in a sexual way.

He moved, loping with a sensual ease, and her fingers tugged at the ribbons of her chemise, removing them, and sliding the material away before working at the corset she'd chosen, the tiny loops she'd designed allowing her to remove it quickly.

He choked audibly, and she glanced at him. "What?"

"You're killing me, Constance. Watching you undress…"

There was no mistaking the hunger on his face, his face hard and eyes glittering. Nor could she ignore the jut of his erection, freed from the confines of his trousers. Glancing at the length, she swallowed. "Is that going to fit?"

"Oh God, yes it will. But how about we get you out of your petticoat and drawers so I can show you how?"

She'd never been shy, but seeing him in all his glory? Oh my, but he is built like a warrior. And when he crowded close, unfastened the cord holding her petticoat and slid it down her legs, she shivered a little.

"Don't be afraid. I won't hurt you," he whispered as if he read her deepest fear.

"I..." She banished the terror of remembering, focusing on the soft touches he gifted her while removing the last fabric barrier between them.

"I'm going to kiss you. Every touch will bring pleasure, Constance. Just lie back," he said, and with a gentle hand, he propelled her backward so she lay before him.

With careful moves, he opened her legs so he could stand between them, and she felt the nudge of his body against her most secret recesses. When he bent forward, the whisper of his breath drove her senses wild, and she quivered beneath him.

His tongue dragged over the tip of her breast, and she arched up, crying out his name. "Feel the pleasure. My lips, my tongue, and my breath heating you. You're warming up, aren't you? Feeling the fire here," he said, and his fingers drew a slow circle over her belly. "And here." They slid lower to the soft, downy-covered folds.

"I..." Words were impossible as he continued winding his magic around her, kissing then lightly blowing on her nipples, softly squeezing before his other hand delved between her thighs and found the tiny, hidden nub, toyed with it, and she was lost. Driven by the heat and emptiness that demanded more.

Her fingers twined in the bedclothes, desperate for purchase when all other reality was burned away under his movements. "Matteo," she cried out as a finger slid inside her.

"So hot and wet. So ready," he crooned and moved.

Pressure built as his hips moved slowly, incrementally invading her body in a way she'd not understood.

Her breath caught, and he moved a little more. "God, Constance, I want you," he growled.

"Please," she entreated, and he moved once more. A hard, savage thrust.

Pain. Sharp and stinging.

She cried out, tried to move away, but his fingers dug into her hips. "Wait," he demanded. "It will pass. Soon."

Tears burned. "You said pleasure," she called, broken in that second.

"Yes, but first the pain, sweetheart. Just for a moment. It will ease." He gazed at her, his face hard. "I promise."

Then it was easing, and she could breathe freely again. "Pleasure? This isn't..."

"Shhh," he whispered. "Let me show you."

"No, I don't think so," she muttered, but he shook his head and nudged his hips.

She gasped now, as a new sensation filled her. Heat. Pleasure.

"See?" His smile was voracious. "Lie back and let me show you about pleasure." He nudged again while his hands left her hips. "Your breasts are perfect. Your nipples like raspberries fresh from the bush, and your body is exquisite. Curved in all the right places," he crooned. "I noticed that the first time I saw you, that you're perfectly proportioned. Your legs are long enough to wind around my waist. Go on, grab me tight so your thighs mount my hips."

Without a sound, she followed his instructions and felt the deepening pleasure winding inside, like a wire pulled taut.

Breath fled as they both moved, flexing and sliding, the sounds of love filling the air. "Oh God, sweetheart. You're so tight," he groaned, and she reached out and up, gripping his shoulders, letting her body dictate what she needed.

Then she was on a precipice, her body coiled, and her fingers gripped hard, nails cutting into flesh.

"Let go, love. I'll catch you," he muttered.

And she did. Then her mind splintered under the sensual onslaught.

Chapter Fourteen

MATTEO WOKE SLOWLY; the feeling of well-being and the warmth keeping him under the depths of sleep scattered as a blonde hair tickled his nose.

He bolted upright and inhaled sharply, because he remembered everything. Every sigh and every touch.

Constance. What have I done? The brutal truth was he'd taken her innocence, and while she had met him passion for passion, there was no denying the truth.

He squeezed his eyes shut, feeling shame cascade.

He'd offered her nothing more than a short liaison. He'd told her that without saying the words. He'd made no promises of love or marriage. The truth was, he was little more than a cad. A bounder. No better than the rest of the men of Casa Bonita.

"Matteo, you're not supposed to be frowning, are you?" Her voice, still sleepy, cut through the self-recriminations.

"What I did last night was unconscionable." He stared into her beautiful eyes. "I took something that wasn't mine to take." The truth was scouring.

With a hand on the sheet, she slid upward so she sat beside him. "Matteo, we both agreed. There's no agreement between us, except the pleasure. You told me that, and I agreed. What you have, I gave freely." She sighed and cupped his cheek. "You gave me a gift, Matteo. Yourself. I don't take that lightly, and to be honest, I'm not sure either of us is either prepared or whole enough to know what to do with a future." She shrugged.

He laughed, a jagged sound. "I'm damaged by Casa Bonita, but you have—"

"A whole history that regularly reminds me of my past. Memories and nightmares."

He frowned, hating to hear the words coming from her mouth. A mouth that brought him such pleasure. "But Damien and Amaryllis—"

"They gave me love and a future, but before... Before my mother died, I saw things, heard things, and experienced things no child should."

"Who?" Fury rose. "Who hurt you?"

She shook her head. "He's dead, but like you, like the scars on your back, I'm not whole, Matteo. For years I hid from myself, but at night, there's no ignoring the truth. But I've come to terms with that. Tell me though, how did you get..." She waved at his back.

"A long time ago, there was a boy who saw things happen to his sister. Things that he should have kept her safe from."

"You?"

He nodded, swallowing his distress as he considered the memory. "She was so young, and so beautiful. Her name was Nadia. She was sixteen, Constance." He sighed, wishing the past could be undone, not for the first time. "One of the men, a council member, he wanted her. He petitioned my father who granted her in marriage. She didn't want him. He broke her body and spirit."

He looked up at her now, needing her to understand what drove him daily.

"I saw her a couple of months after the marriage," he continued. "She was pale and gaunt. A shadow, I guess, of who and what she'd been. I tried to get to her, to get her away. They found us, she was pregnant so she'd been ill, and we were too slow. We were almost at the boat when we were cornered." He closed his eyes, hating the sounds she'd made, and the rough handling she endured because he'd failed her. Years had passed, and still, the sound haunted him.

"What happened to you after that?" Her fingers touched his hand, and he held on, gripped hard, needing her to centre him.

"I was whipped in the square. I had to be made an example of. 'This is what happens when you interfere in the will of the master,' he said. My father." Bitterness dripped from Matteo's words. "He was no father, not to me nor any of the others. When we were old enough, he had us taken from our mothers, placed in a bunkhouse. Fight or die was our motto. Plenty did." He shook his head. "What kind of monster does that?"

"But you knew your sister?"

He laughed, a bitter shard of sound. "When we were sick, then our mothers were permitted to care for us. That's the only way most of us knew who'd birthed us. Most of the other boys were cold toward their mothers. Mine was... soft. Loving. She wished things were different, that she could raise me. The only mother permitted to keep her child was his first wife. The one who'd sired his first son, my brother, Javier."

Her hand slid over his cheek, and he felt surprised when his own tears smeared.

"Fathers don't do that," she said. "They don't separate child from mother or make them into cold, unfeeling brutes. We came from evil, both of us, Matteo. We both made choices that brought us here. We both stand for good, that's why we do what we do."

He dropped his head, humbled, because while he'd not really considered that they both had experiences which scarred them, she hadn't allowed that past to fill her with hate or grief. He'd been so immersed, wallowing in his emotions, he'd failed to understand. He'd been blinded, and for that he was ashamed.

He leaned in, kissed her gently. "You're far too giving, Constance. It's both a failing and a blessing."

She laughed then. "Maybe, but I think we've both weathered enough storms to know it's the hard times that give us the strength to keep going." She sighed, her gaze flicking to the window covered by a curtain. "But keeping going means we need to go about our daily routines." Her face clouded. "I have suits to make, arrangements too, and…" She shrugged. "…furniture to order."

Constance felt Matteo's gaze on her back as she left the room, and if she could, she'd go back and give them more time. But that wasn't in their future.

She hadn't understood, not until now, that her emotions would be engaged after the fact. "I guess that makes sense, just look at Ammy and Damien or Frannie and Raphael."

She shook her head; it was time to learn that not every intimate encounter was what she'd remembered. Sometimes gentleness—as she'd seen with her sister and adoptive parents—was part of intimacy. It was the reason she'd been prepared to take a chance, because cruelty and debasement didn't figure in those relationships. She'd learned that first-hand last night, hadn't she?

Walking into the bedroom she'd taken as her own, she changed quickly, after washing her body. Funny how sensitive parts of her body felt.

"Come on, you have things to do," she told herself.

In the dining area she spied Matteo waiting for her as she emerged from her chamber. She moved toward him.

"You should eat, Constance," he told her, and she had a flash of the night before, consuming a quick meal before returning to her task and him urging her to take a break.

"You're looking after me, are you, Matteo?"

He grinned. "If you'll let me."

God knew she'd let him because something had unfurled overnight. An emotion she wasn't ready to call love, but it felt deep and abiding. "Only until I leave," she answered, because that sudden knowledge terrified her.

His glance at her was warm. "Here, have some oatmeal."

She laughed. "No one has fed me oatmeal in years."

"It's good for you. Helps to get you through the day." He spooned some into his bowl from the pot, then passed it to her. "Sugar? Syrup?"

Adding a generous portion of the oats, she considered his offer. "No, I think plain will be fine today."

They ate in companionable silence, and when she was done, she rose.

"I need to work," she stated, and he nodded his agreement.

"So do I. James is meeting with Felix today. He left last night for the coast."

"Oh. Do you think you'll have answers today?" She squinted down at her gown, realising in her haste she'd missed a button.

"Let me," he said and reached out to fasten it. "I don't think so. Not unless Felix has a brother or sister close to Javier. My brother isn't the trusting sort. He's cold and strategic, so letting anyone he doesn't fully trust into his inner circle, let alone telling them what he was planning, would be too great a risk."

"Oh," she answered. "That makes sense. I mean, both Damien and Raphael guard us closely. And talking about guards, I think my father is due today or tomorrow."

Matteo's shoulders slumped. "Then I believe that we shouldn't revisit last night again."

She cocked her head, surprised by his suggestion. "Why? He'll likely stay overnight on the dirigible."

"He'll want you to stay with him, won't he?"

Constance tapped her finger to her lips. "I don't think so. Not if I tell him I have tasks that need to be completed. Besides, I wouldn't be surprised if Anderton hasn't been apprising him of my schedule. He's going ahead to meet my father, taking the automotive to him."

When Matteo grunted, she smiled. "He's very modern in outlook. He and Ammy married after... you know, they were intimate."

He appeared shocked. "How do you know that?"

"I wasn't a baby, you know. When we travelled to the island, I was old enough to understand. I got up one night, looking for Ammy, and she wasn't in her room. I heard them. Damien and Ammy." She shrugged. "I knew what they were doing, I'd seen my mother and him. *My father*," she clarified, and a wealth of loathing betrayed her emotional response to her birth parents.

His hand touched hers, and the warmth of his touch melted the ice that seemed to fill her whenever she remembered the past deeds.

He tugged her close, kissed her gently. "Thank you."

"For what?" What had she done that made him thank her?

"For being you, Constance." Now he stepped away. "Go work. I'll be in soon," he said, then left the room.

Chapter Fifteen

THREE DAYS LATER…

JAMES' short communication hadn't surprised Matteo as he rose from the communicase. The large wood and copper unit's light flashed off, and he sunk his hands into the pockets of his trousers.

All he'd learned was there was movement, but no detail. More men had left the island. People were moving, and James would return later in the day.

Javier always played it close to his chest, but surely there should be some kind of indication?

Matteo made his way to the office and noted that Constance was standing by some kind of lifelike statue, fiddling with the material, but it was clearly now a jacket, high-necked and the arms extending to a point.

"You've been busy," he stated.

She turned, a smile on her face. "You're here. Excellent. Let me see how the jacket fits, then all we need to do is finalise fasteners. The trousers are nearly done too. Do you prefer a belt, or would suspenders work better?"

He blinked. "Suspenders?"

"The suit is designed to allow for movement, so the waist is higher than usual. It allows for greater movement."

"Huh." He inspected the jacket. "Is it heavy?"

"Not really. Here, take off your jacket and try it on," she said, sliding the garment from the stand.

He removed his jacket, took the item from her hands, and slid it on. It was comfortable, heavier than a usual jacket, but the fabric itself moved with him.

She wrapped the front section over right over left. "Buttons will be secure but harder to get off, if necessary, in a hurry. I could place buckles on it if you prefer?" She moved away, slid her hand into a bag, and tugged out a small, copper buckle. "Like this. I think four would be enough with a button at the throat." She inspected the buckle against the dark brown fabric. "What do you think?"

The sight of her was entrancing. "You are amazing," he said, and she blushed.

"Not really." She ducked away.

He tugged off the jacket. "You shouldn't brush off compliments, Constance. This is amazing."

"Ah, well, it's a skill, yes. Now, pants time." She raised an eyebrow, and a seed of devilry took hold of him.

His hands found the belt buckle and he undid it, his gaze holding hers as she watched him. The buttons of his trousers posed no barrier either, and he reached further, finding the string of his underwear and loosening them at the same time, then slid the material to the ground.

A flush coloured her cheeks while she toyed with the button at her throat. "No, leave it," he ordered.

Her mouth formed an 'oh' as he kicked off his pants, then stalked over, grabbed her up, and marched with her to his desk. "I wonder how you'd look fully clothed while I love you? Will you get heated and your hair tumble?"

He loved the sight of her surprise, followed by the impish smile.

"Well, I don't know, as I've no experience," she breathed. "Perhaps you should let me experience it?"

God knew she was like a drug, and once he'd had her, he was addicted.

He laid her on the desk, lifted her skirt, and found she wore a light petticoat and drawers that were so fine as to be almost see-through. "Pretty underthings, good thing I won't rip them," he said, and she bit her lip.

His body jerked; he was already rigid and ready. His hands traced over the dips and raises covered by the material. "Soft," he said, and she squirmed. "Be still, Constance. Stay still and let me show you wonder."

"No, don't... don't play with me," she muttered, and he couldn't help but smile. She too was engaged in what they were doing.

"Play with you—how I'd like that. Next time we'll play and dance. But now? I need you, Constance, just like you need me. I can feel your heat." His fingers quested for the ribbon, loosened it, and released her.

The air around them was full of the scent of sex, and he inhaled. Let the heady fragrance fill his mind as he slid the material from her body, over the light shoes, and onto the floor behind him.

She was bared to his sight, and his fingers played with her, sliding between her damp, fleshy lips, toying with her clitoral bud, until she arched up, cried out.

His finger found her entrance, slid in ever so slowly. "Feel me, Constance. Know that I'm inside you, testing you, preparing you."

Matteo's loins ached with the pressure of arousal, and every moan and move she made added to his own.

"Please, Matteo. Come to me," she urged, and he stepped forward, bent down, and kissed her lightly where they would soon join.

"Yes," he said, then stood and slid in, slow and steady, as measured as he could bear, though the beat of his own need urged him to move faster and wilder. To show her how much pleasure they brought each other.

Her legs clasped him, surrounding his hips, and held him close as she joined the wild dance. Moving and clutching, needing, and fulfilling.

He felt the moment her body slid over the edge, and he followed, his hands gripping her tightly to him as he filled her.

The drumbeat of his heart stuttered at the realisation of just how over-his-head he was. He wanted her day and night. Needed her, not like a drug but more as the other half of himself. His fingers bit deep into her skin.

"Ow," she exclaimed. "Matteo? Are you all right?"

He pulled away, regret gnawing at him. He'd been on her like a rutting bull, and she'd been compliant... Like the women of the houses were meant to be. Used. Abandoned.

"Jesus," he whispered. "I..."

She sat up. "Matteo?"

"I'm no better than them, am I?" He sighed, feeling a weariness deep in his soul. "I..." He found his clothing and begin to dress quickly, shame filling him.

"Matteo, wait!" Constance called, but he hurried through the task. "Matteo! I was an equal partner." He heard her movements, felt when her hand settled on his shoulder. "Don't treat me like I'm some kind of victim."

He turned. "But that's exactly—"

"No!" She shook her head. "I'm a fully grown woman, who makes her own decisions. Don't make me into a saint or a martyr, because I'm neither. I wanted you. Hell, I still do. But I also know that what we have has an..." He watched as she clearly struggled to find the word to describe their situation. "An expiry date. When I leave here, we'll be done. I know that. You told me that, and I still agreed."

"I seduced you," he stated bluntly.

"Oh, please? You think so little of me that you believe fancy words will make me open my legs?"

He flinched at her crude description. "Constance..."

"You've had long enough to wallow in whatever emotional cesspit is inside your head. But now it's time to listen. I'm not your sister. I choose who I take as a lover, and I chose you." Her voice softened. "I chose you, Matteo. Don't make me regret it."

She turned away, and her shoulders slumped, and he covered his face with a hand. "I just... I should have treated you like a lady."

The sadness on her face as she looked over her shoulder spoke volumes. "I want you to treat me like me, Matteo." A long moment passed, then she sighed. "You should try the pants on. Tell me what you want so I can complete yours, then I guess, I'll wait for my father."

It was a dismissal and it cut. Deep. "Constance?"

"Please. I... I need to finish, then I have things to do."

Chapter Sixteen

CONSTANCE MET her father at the door. "Damien!"

He held her tight, and she snuggled in, needing the encouragement and love. She'd been bruised by her latest encounter with Matteo. Was this what loving was like? The ups and downs that cut at her?

"What's wrong, Connie?" He pulled away to scan her face.

"Nothing. I mean... How did you know—with Ammy?"

His face fell. "That's why you've decided on here? Matteo?"

She shook her head, but knew he'd read the confusion. "I... I don't know what to do. He doesn't want me, not now, because his focus is Casa Bonita. I always said..." she choked the words out. "I never wanted love. Children were never a focus for me."

Her father tugged her into a seat beside him, holding tight to her hands. "Why?"

It was time to tell him. Time to explain the things she'd held deep inside. "I... Before my birth father died, he would do things."

She felt the sudden calmness about him, as if he was preparing himself for a blow. "What?"

"He'd stand in the doorway and watch me. He'd... He'd do things to himself and call me his little wife. It felt wrong and dirty. Then he'd go to mother, and I'd watch, because he told me..." She swallowed. "...if I didn't, he'd do that to Faith. I had to protect her. I knew it was wrong." She shuddered. "When he died, I was glad, but Mother, she grew ill and there was no one to help us. Not until your sister, then you and Amaryllis."

"You never said. Frannie…"

"He hated her, so she was safe. But me? He had plans for me. He said when I was old enough, he'd ensure I had the right preparation, and he'd find the right husband. One malleable to…" Her hands clenched into fists. "I was prepared to fight him, Damien. But at night, when I slept, it would come back to me, and I'd see him in my dreams. See him. Hear all the horrible things he promised. The way he'd smile at me, then touch himself."

He hugged her tight. "He was an evil man, Constance. The things he said and did…"

"I know," she said. "I learned from you and Ammy and Frannie and Raphael, but inside, I don't think I'm ever going to be right. I feel like part of me is tainted, and no matter what I do, or how hard…" The words felt like boulders, but the need to expel them from her mind was too great. "I felt like I had nothing worthwhile until now. I learned something about myself during this time with Matteo. I learned I can do good things and be a force for change."

"Constance, you've always been a source of joy to me. A daughter who gave freely, and I never knew…"

"I didn't want you to know. When I was little, I thought if you knew you'd hate me. Send me away. Over the years I've learned control and—"

Damien sighed. "It's a burden you could have shared with me, or both of us. We love you, Constance."

"I know. But now that you know you might understand why my plan is important, why I feel strongly this is the place I need to be. Look at these women and children." She pointed across the yard. "Yes, they have safety, but how will they feed their children? Where is there hope? You gave me that, Damien. You and Ammy together. I need to share it."

His nod was slow but determined. "Then show me what you have found, and we'll find a way to make it work."

She slipped her hand into his. "Thank you," she said, and together they rose.

Matteo was pleased she nor Damien had seen her. He'd heard the words and bile rose. That creature who'd tormented her, the man who'd sired her, was sick.

He heard the words she'd spoken about being pleased the man was dead, but in that moment, Matteo wished he wasn't so he could make the bastard pay. She'd hinted to him about the depth of horrors, but not the full story.

It reinforced to him that the houses brought no joy, only pain. The ones who paid the price were the innocent and the women. "I have to stop it," he told himself and looked to the sky for some kind of divine assistance. It wasn't forthcoming.

A commotion sounded, and he moved toward the man running in his direction. James! "What are you...?"

"I sent for the automotive. Matteo, there's an uprising at Casa Bonita. One of the boats was seen leaving late last night. After I met with Felix, I talked to the harbour master. He said it was full of women and one man—Javier. Another boat, something large, maybe a barquentine, intercepted the vessel, and they went on board. There was gunfire too, but no one could get close enough to investigate."

The words jolted Matteo, and he cursed, having downgraded the security here just yesterday. He'd been so sure... "Get the compound locked up."

"What about Constance? She just left in the automotive with Anderton and Damien Whitmore." James' words speared him.

"Damn it!" He shook his head, because terror inched through him. Constance outside the safety of the compound, with only a single guard and her father. She needed to return to his side. "It's too dangerous—"

"I doubt they know where we are, Matteo. The compound should be safe for a few days."

"No, if she's outside the compound, she's not safe. I need—"

"*Your people need you, Matteo.* She has her father, her guard, and the crew of the Phoenix and whichever craft he came in on." James' hard words didn't soothe him, but they did remind him that he had responsibilities.

He rubbed his hand through his hair. What should be the first directive? "Get the people inside the gates, then close them. Send out the alert to those in town, any that wish to return can. At least the temporary housing is ready."

"We'll need more supplies," James reminded him.

Maybe if he could send a message to Constance? Send her to retrieve them and she stayed away…

"Matteo? Come on, man. Focus. Too many people are relying on you," James said, shoving him hard in the chest.

"You're right," he said, but even as they headed for the office, thoughts and plans whirled around inside his head.

The trip into Bald Head was short, but in that time, it was clear something had occurred, noted Constance. Even before they entered the township, they passed men, women, and children moving on foot in the direction of the compound.

"Anderton? What's happening? Did I miss…?"

"I have no idea, Constance. I know when we left, the residents were on alert, but…" Anderton turned to watch the tide of humanity. "Perhaps Matteo has heard something more on his brother? The men were chattering last night in the bunkhouse, saying that Javier's injuries were likely a blind, to cover some major scandal. But this? I simply don't know enough."

Damien steered the automotive to a smooth stop beside the building she'd named as the prospective work and living space. "Well, we should go in. Take a look around." But he wasn't unaffected either, as Constance noted he reached into a storage lockbox and retrieved an actinic pistol from within, then passed both herself and Anderton pistols.

"I've holsters in the rear storage compartment, but I'd rather not open it just yet."

She blinked. "Why?"

He smiled, and she saw the cold glint. "It's got quite a bit of armament in it, my dear. It wouldn't be wise to alert anyone to the range of rifles and other goodies until we know it's safe."

"You honestly believe that the threat is that great?" Her mouth dried.

"I don't trust any house, Constance. Experience shows me that anytime there is upheaval, the only ones who suffer are those unable to bring order to the chaos."

Anderton nodded. "Yes, I would agree with that. So, it's my opinion we should get ourselves inside, undertake the inspection, then head to a more secure location."

Constance couldn't say she liked what either man was saying, but she refused to let fear stop her from achieving what she'd planned. She exited the automotive and moved to the door of the building, but not without noting the way both Anderton and Damien flanked her once they too had climbed from the vehicle. Damien took the rear position after locking the entry to the automotive, and Anderton used the key they'd obtained just yesterday to open the building's door.

Inside, the building was musty, having been abandoned in the last twelve months. Dust motes danced in the air, and piles of fluff littered the floor, but the large windows ensured the space was light. The white painted walls rose high, and she stepped inside.

"This area would be the shop, though I'd partition the front from the back," she stated. "The windows at the front would be ideal for placing examples into. Mass produced, but more than serviceable, gowns, skirts, and blouses." She pointed to the currently boarded-up glass facing the street. "As we move back, there would be a warehouse area. Bolts of fabric, notions, and of course, completed articles. I don't think that accessories will factor for me, or at least not at this time, as I don't have the expertise nor the space."

"Perhaps at a later date, you could employ someone and move into another local building to provide those items," Damien said.

"Moving further back, there's several big rooms." She led the way, her footsteps echoing as billows of dust flew up. "This one would be an excellent manufactory room. It's big enough that rows of machines could be set up. Another area over there," she said as she waved toward the far side, "a cutting area. Another for finishing work."

"Yes, I see there is plenty of room. How many staff do you envisage?" Damien enquired.

"I think in the first instance, twenty women on machines, four on cutting, two to curate, and another one for warehouse duties. Five on finishing work. At least two in the office. Five in the store, so the service is personalised," Constance answered.

"You mentioned a classroom?" Damien reminded her.

"The classroom is the first room which will need to be completed. I don't know how many women here can sew, so I would need to assess their skill levels. There is likely the need to teach them advanced stitches, to ensure the quality of their work is adequate." Constance entered a room to the left. "This room is the one I thought would meet my needs. Again, it has the windows." She indicated the soaring wall of glass. "I can dress the bottom, so their privacy is guaranteed, but it won't obscure the lights. Oh, and I thought to fit the building with photonic lighting."

Damien smiled. "Keeping that fit out in the family? I'm sure I can direct the Igneous Corporation to ship and fit free of charge. We'll explain it to the bean counters as a marketing opportunity."

Constance smiled. "Well, it's a good thing you own the business then, isn't it, Father?"

He laughed, a loud guffaw. "Come, show me the rest."

She did, and in short order they were mounting the stairs to what would become her living area. "I was thinking another staircase to the rear, and perhaps one near the front."

Anderton cleared his throat. "I see people are still moving around outside. Perhaps I should go find out what's happened?"

Damien nodded. "Return as soon as you know."

Anderton left them, and Damien and Constance mounted the circular stairs.

"The bones of the building are solid," he told her. "But my concern was more around its security."

"There's room for several guards, who would remain on-site, and I was thinking of purchasing some houses, to employ the daytime contingent. Perhaps three shifts, so none of them are working more than eight hours." Constance sighed. "Security isn't my strong suit, so I don't know how many…" She shrugged.

"Yes, I understand that. We could offset that by purchasing two or three of the buildings abutting. Then you can have your security teams vet tenants. Put in place extra security teams."

"Anderton suggested something similar, so I had him enquire as to the costs." She named it and watched as Damien visibly winced. "Yes, and that chunk of my start-up costs—"

"Yes, I see. However, there would be an almost immediate income, as I see there are businesses in most of the buildings," he countered.

"Yes. And they are all solid buildings of brick construction. Anderton was pleased with that and said they were more easily secured than wooden structures," she said, and Damien nodded his agreement. "Plus, it was the same developer who built them, so he thinks there may be some room to negotiate, as it would be a large purchase. In cash."

They stopped at the top of the stairs, and Damien's gaze swept the main room. "Impressive. Show me the rest."

They took their time as Constance outlined her vision for the living space. A large parlour, formal dining room and family version. The kitchen area was poor, but until she found someone to cook for her, she needed little. Then the area could be completely refitted as needed. There was space for a main suite, complete with a private bath and dressing area. Three more bedrooms with a central bathroom, then at the rear, a series of small, private rooms with central bathing facilities for the staff, and a private common room.

"Well?" Constance felt the butterflies in her stomach dancing around.

"You've chosen well. The set-up costs will be large, and it will take some time before you're turning a profit, but with the multiple arms of manufacturing, sales, and teaching, it's sound. We should meet with the developer and see what can be negotiated."

She released the breath she'd been holding, the tension in her body washing away. "Thank you, Father."

He smiled. "I'm proud of you, Constance. This is a good, solid plan, and you've done well. I just wish…" His smile dimmed a little.

"What?"

"I wish you were nearer us. But we can visit regularly, and I'll have a communicase fitted in your office and a private one in your residence too."

The gates were closed, the sea of people having migrated to the compound, yet there was no sign of Constance, Damien, or Anderton. Matteo rose and moved to the communicase, pressed in the individual address of the Phoenix communicator, and waited.

"*Phoenix Dirigible* here," came the scratchy voice of the captain.

"Matteo Bonita. Have you any sign of Damien Whitmore, his daughter, and her guard?" His fingers curled around the receiver as he waited on the answer.

"No, sir. However, I could send men to make enquiries. Is there some specific request you'd like them to make?" The captain had no idea what was going on, but then, why would he? Matteo squeezed his eyes shut.

"I need them to return to the compound. There's a security breach and—"

"Security breach? Sir, we're miles from anywhere," the man blustered, and Matteo felt the rise of his blood pressure.

"Send for them, Captain. Once your men have delivered the message, contact me with a location update." Breaking the connection, he slumped in the chair.

"Did you get hold of her?" James' voice came from the doorway.

"No, I got the captain. He has no idea of the danger." The genuine lack of concern ate at Matteo, but he turned the chair on the wheel to face his friend. "You were right, though, earlier. I have responsibilities. So, what's the latest news from Casa Bonita?"

He knew that Felix had agreed to pass on any information, as had the harbour master, and James wouldn't have darkened his office door without reason. Not after what James said earlier in the day to him.

. . .

They retreated inside, and James grabbed him, stopped him from stalking off. "You must get it together. People are relying on you, damn it, Matteo. People who could still lose everything if you aren't awake."

He mumbled, "I'm worried."

James' features softened. "I know. But at least she's got protection. They've only got us. When they followed us, we promised that we'd keep them and their families safe. A promise they believed. They came here expecting you to provide what they need."

Matteo nodded, shame filling him. "You're right, but that doesn't negate..." His shrug was slow. "But I must make plans. I know. I'll try and raise the captain. Get word to them. Meanwhile, check the food situation, let me know how many days we're able to cater. Water too."

James slapped him on the back in a gesture that told him the other man truly understood.

"We've got enough food stock for around six weeks. Water barrels enough that with our average use, five and a half weeks. The well is also nearly full, so that will give us time. On the Casa Bonita front, there's been full boats of men leaving the island. The harbour master said there had to be two-to-three hundred leaving. They were taking wagon loads, fully laden."

"Where to?" Matteo needed to know more. Too many questions. Not enough answers.

"No one seems to know." But James' eyes told a different story.

"What?" Damien demanded.

"Well, if we work out the shortest direct route..."

"How many days to here?" he growled, and James held up three fingers.

"But only if they walk. We know Javier had other men, on the mainland, watching. If they've been prepared, they could be here sooner. Within a day if they are on horseback. Less using an automotive."

Matteo's eyes closed as he considered the information. "They'll head into town. Look to gather their own information." Opening his eyes, he pinned his friend with a stare. "They'll know about Constance. That she was here and looking to purchase."

"The only building which would suit any kind of long-term plan is the old mercantile. It's a solid building, Matteo."

"I want her here, James."

His friend's gaze turned mournful, and it reminded Matteo of what they'd both lost to Casa Bonita. Matteo's sister and James' betrothed. "I agree. She'd be a target."

"Damn it all," he roared.

Chapter Seventeen

ANDERTON RETURNED AT A RUN. "They've closed the compound gates, and there's a group of men in at least five automotives heading in this direction. They're flying the flag of Casa Bonita."

Constance gulped down the fear which rose in her throat. "We should head—"

"To the Phoenix." Damien nodded. "It's defensible."

Even as they headed out the door, a plume of dust in the near distance caught Constance's eye. "I think we're too late," she whispered and pointed. "I think they're already here."

James entered the office. "They're here, Matteo. The torches in town have been lit!"

Matteo surged up from the seat. "How? When?"

"Just now. The lights on the beacons are now flying." James' eyes were wild. "What do we...?"

Matteo didn't need to think. They'd practiced and prepared for so long for this eventuality, that he acted as necessary without thought. "Man the barriers, women and children into the bunkers."

For a moment, fear gripped him for Constance, but there was little he could do for her right now. He ached, but the faces turned in his direction reminded him that he was the leader of this group. He'd donned the suit she'd finished for him just yesterday and tugged on the mask she'd insisted he take from the trunk.

"Father insisted I keep the first one, but I think you should have it. While it's not been tested in battle, we ran tests in the ballistic laboratory." Her eyes glinted. "Since it's made with the ballistafabric, it should keep you safe."

He cupped her cheek. "Constance, I'm overwhelmed."

This time when she smiled, a hint of a dimple emerged in her cheek. "I do my best," she whispered.

"Why?"

"Why do I do my best? Or why did I give it to you?" She tapped her finger to her lips. "Let me think. It could be because I want you to be safe. It could be because I think you'll look charming in it..." She laughed. "It could be to thank you." Her smile died away. "I need to know you'll survive. You've given me something of value, and I'd like to keep you around a little longer so I can appreciate you more."

"Constance, I'm..." He shrugged. "Thank you." There didn't seem to be much else to say.

"Just wear it, and that's all the thanks I need, Matteo." Then she kissed him again.

"I'm going up to the crow's nest. I need to see for myself what's coming," Matteo said as he brushed past James.

His friend caught his arm. "I'll come with you."

Matteo shook his head. "I've got the ballistafabric suit and Constance's mask. You stay here." He strode off and headed to the ladder leaned up near the front gates. Climbing to the top, he looked out.

Vehicles were moving quickly, but he couldn't miss the armaments pointed in the direction of the gates. He hoped the reinforcements he'd made to the walls would keep them all safe; he'd spent almost a fortune on it to ensure the safety of those seeking shelter within.

The cloud rose in the distance, but he noted they headed for the town. His guts seized. Surely Damien would get her to the Phoenix before it was too late?

The struggle to separate the man from the leader took long seconds. Should he go to her? But the people—

"Matteo? What do we do?" one of the men who'd been in the crow's nest asked.

Matteo grabbed the nearest pole, the sting of the wood biting into his hands. "We protect what's ours." He swung back to look at the compound, those gathered within, terror on their faces. "Our families need us to be strong. Keep an eye out. They appear to be headed for the town, but that will only hold them for so long." He refused to turn around, because the pain squeezing his chest was too much. "We protect the compound."

Damien shoved Constance inside the building. "Do you have your suit?"

She nodded. "In the vehicle."

Damien sent Anderton to retrieve it and the armaments he'd stored in the trunk. As people ran by, he called them in, and they entered the building, terror etched on their faces, blank eyes. Pale skin.

The streets were empty as the first vehicle plunged into the road, and Damien and Anderton shoved the door shut. "Close the shutters," he bellowed, and Constance led the charge.

"Quick, help me shut them," she called, and those capable scurried out, closing the heavy wooden and metal covers, while Damien and Anderton laid out the weapons.

Once the task was completed, he called them together, and while Constance watched, he checked those within for skills that may prove useful. Those with security and guard experience were sent upstairs with rifles and handguns of various kinds. Some had medical experience. Others would attend to the children gathered.

It was a small knot of people who'd been too slow to make it to the compound; maybe thirty men, women, and children. When Anderton handed Constance the suit, she sighed, retreated to one of the smaller inner rooms, and dressed quickly, leaving her normal clothes in a pool on the floor.

Her father waited. "Where's the mask?"

Constance gulped. "I gave it to Matteo. I thought he'd need it more than I would," she whispered, and Damien's face darkened.

"Constance, it wasn't meant for Matteo, it was meant for you—"

"I know, but I didn't think I'd need it. Now what?" Constance inhaled a steady breath. They'd need to concentrate to get through this mess.

"Here." Damien thrust an aether rifle into her hand.

The weapon's examination took no time, and she looked up. "Where?"

"The roof. You're a bad shot, but at least up there you might hit one of the vehicles," Damien muttered, and she released a tiny, rough laugh.

"At least you're honest," she murmured and turned on her heel, making her way to the steps in the centre of the building.

"Constance?" Damien's call had her turning back. "Take care up there. No daft chance taking."

She nodded and headed up the metal steps, noting the clangs of her footsteps. At the top of the building, she stilled, found the doorknob, and opened it to step onto the roof.

Not having inspected this area, she was surprised to note the height of the building walls were higher than the roof. "Gives me a chance to hide," she muttered as she crept toward the edge and peered over carefully.

The vehicles had formed a line in the middle of the road, men with rifles peering up and down the road, while those in the lead vehicle climbed slowly out, and others scurried toward them.

She wished she'd thought to ask for spy glasses, but without any, she took a chance, crept along the length of the roof to the very corner as the dampness of her palms reminded her of the danger of the situation.

The man talking was large, well-built, and for the first time, she thought someone else was within the lead car. Someone slight. Was it...a woman?

Constance rubbed her eyes as the figure slid across the seat, and one foot, then another emerged.

The man hurried back, reached in, and assisted her to rise, handing her an item he'd taken from the vehicle.

She frowned because it looked like a... walking stick.

"What's going on?" Constance whispered, watching as the woman peered up and down the street, her free hand moving animatedly.

Constance would have given anything to know what the woman was saying, and she reached onto her tiptoes. As she did, a brick shifted, teetered, and fell with a crash to the ground below. Close to the small knot.

Constance jumped back in time to avoid the 'phut' of an actinic rifle discharge; it shot upward where she'd been peering over the edge. Sweat drenched her, and she crouched on the floor where she'd landed, and she glared at the hole in the masonry. "Stupid," she muttered while yells and bellows echoed from below.

The roof door smashed open, and she glanced around to see Damien and Anderton run toward her. "Constance!" bellowed her father.

"I'm... I'm okay," she answered, feeling both foolish and chastened.

"What the hell did you do?" Damien's furious question left Constance burning with embarrassment.

"Nothing! I was looking over the edge and a brick came free. It landed..." Before she could complete the sentence, a banging echoed from below.

Rifle fire! Anderton made his way carefully to the edge. "We've got problems. They're trying to get in through the main door," he growled.

"So how do we...?"

"Send the people out the back. Tell them to seek shelter in the nearer buildings. In basements and anywhere they can hide." Damien's voice was a snarl. "Then we need to get to the Phoenix."

Constance bolted upright. "What?" She pushed off the floor. "No. We have a duty to help these people."

"They aren't your people, Constance," Damien reminded her.

She shook her head. "Not yet, but they could be. I'm not leaving them to fend for themselves. Don't ask me to do that, Damien." Her heart pounded as she waited for his response.

He sighed. "I had to check. Fine then, we get them out of here and find a bolt-hole until we can safely get them to the compound. Or..." Damien glanced toward the port, where the two dirigibles waited. "We get them out of here."

She glanced at the sky. "What time is it?"

Damien grunted, then checked his chronograph. "Nearing two in the afternoon."

Biting her lip, Constance considered the situation. "There's probably four or five hours until the sun goes down."

"If we stay here that long, we won't get out," Damien said.

"No, you're right. But we need them to find a place for a few hours. Somewhere to hide. Then they come together after dark in a location. We send people to them then, to meet them, get them to safety."

He frowned. "There's a lot of unknowns in that."

She shrugged. "It's all I've got, unless you have—"

Damien sighed. "No, that's more than I have." He glanced down, and she hated that he looked defeated.

"Damien?"

"I'm too old for this stuff. I've got soft," he muttered.

She laughed. "Maybe so, but right now, I'm pleased you're here with me."

They hurried down the steps, Anderton bringing up the rear.

Chapter Eighteen

SUNSET WAS LOOMING as Matteo waited in the crow's nest once more. Still no communications from Damien, Constance, and Anderton. Still no apparent movement from the town.

What the hell is happening?

He peered through the ocular James had found for him, hoping for something more. Earlier in the day several shots had been fired, and the memory of it still dried his mouth.

Climbing down the ladder, the first echo of a shot broke through the air.

The compound became silent, and though Matteo might be halfway down the ladder, he stilled, then scurried back up.

James followed him, a brass ocular swung from a leather strap. "Here," James said as he shoved the item at him.

Peering into it, Matteo noted the cars sitting outside the old mercantile. The same building Constance and Damien had travelled to see. The automotive sat outside, the outer shell covered with a metal exoskeleton he'd noted previously but not really thought about.

"Matteo?"

"They're inside the mercantile. The vehicles outside. I don't..." He

shoved the ocular to James and dragged an unsteady hand through his hair. He could send someone out there, a small contingent, but that would leave the compound undermanned. Unprotected.

Sourness coated his throat.

"Damien will protect her," James said. "He's got quite a reputation, both as a fighter and negotiator."

Matteo glanced back to the building in the far distance. "I just hope that's what they need," he growled.

"And us?"

There was no other choice. "We remain on alert. Until we know what's happening, there's no other option, James. We protect our people."

His best friend nodded, and Matteo backed away and clambered down the ladder to the ground.

One of the women hurried forward and handed him a bowl of something, and while he really wasn't interested, Matteo also understood that it was necessary to feed his body, so he shovelled it in, not taking time to taste anything. When the bowl was empty, he handed it back with a brief, "Thanks," then waited for the woman to leave.

Matteo looked up at the gates and wondered what would happen if he stepped outside. If he made the representation to cease any kind of conflict with those in the town.

He sighed and turned back to James. "We need to make sure we have shifts. Three, I think. Eight hours apiece, so the men are rested. Also, the women. The men will be hungry at different times, so we need to make sure there's adequate food options when the men are hungry. It might be best to see which women without very young children can assist in that area. We standardise the assistance available, pooling the resources of those who've joined us, those in the bunkhouses and those in the big house and the huts."

James' gaze roamed his face. "Are you good?"

Matteo gave a single, quick nod. He had to concentrate on what was going on, rather than allowing his brain to consider the situation with Constance.

He marched over to the long table the men had set up in the middle of the yard so the women could serve foods. The women were moving around the table, setting up flaming torches so the area would be illuminated come night.

"Matteo," one of the women called, and he turned.

"What?"

"It would be better if we could use the photic lighting." She moved from foot to foot, and he understood that asking for him to consider this was huge for her. In the houses, women had no power to affect any kind of change.

"Under normal circumstances, I would agree, Lorraine, but we need to conserve our resources. So, this is the best option we have for the moment." He waited for the understanding to hit.

"Oh. Okay then." She stepped back, gave a nod, and moistened her lips. "Thank... Thank you for explaining."

James sat down with the list of men available for the shifts of security. "I'll have this done quickly," he said, checking the list of those in the compound as well as those from outside the compound.

Matteo waited, his eyes taking in the careful movements of those who'd sought safety. "We have all the details?"

"What? Oh yes. We held them all until we could process them before admitting them. Our men on the gates were on the job fast," James answered.

Matteo grunted. He detested the lack of control over the situation, and he tapped his hand against his legs as he waited.

A call went out, "We've got a vehicle!"

Matteo ran to the ladder. He clambered up it quickly to watch the vehicle's approach.

Constance waited in the dark. They'd left the building with the flood of others, who'd scattered. At sunset, the women and children would converge on the port, but Damien, Constance, and Anderton would be aboard. The plan was for the three of them to start moving in the late afternoon, dodging from one hidden spot to the next until they were within distance of the dirigible. Then they'd signal the crew with flashes of light.

"We don't have a mirror," Damien explained. "So, we think about what we have that is reflective."

Constance frowned. "I don't…"

Anderton shook his head.

Damien smiled. "My pocket chrono has a reflective surface. We use that to catch the attention of the crew."

Constance made a mental note that she should investigate purchasing a small chronograph with a reflective surface, not that she thought she'd ever be in this situation again.

She crouched beside Damien, as he considered where the dying rays of sunlight illuminated the gloom, then began moving the chrono up and down, side to side to capture the rays.

She held her breath, hoping that they'd not begun signalling too late, and kept her eye on the dirigible.

Time passed. It felt like hours before movement began at the gang-plank. Damien hauled her up and, together with Anderton, they sprinted for the ship, up onto the wooden boards of the platform. Finally they were safe.

Her chest bellowed at the sudden exertion, and she turned around, even though Damien was urging her inside. Anderton melted into the background, and she assumed it was to inform the rest of the crew what was about to happen, as others would soon begin to dribble out into the night, seeking their assistance.

The captain joined them. "Sir, I'm so pleased you and Miss Constance are safe. We should ascend immediately…"

"Belay that order, Captain. Contact the Gloriana. Inform the captain we'll both be taking on refugees." Damien's voice echoed in the sudden stillness.

"Captain!" A crew member sped out of the structure and stood panting beside his senior officer. "There's news from the compound. You need to come..."

Damien frowned. "What news?"

The sailor shook his head. "Said it was confidential and only for the captain."

"Then we should go hear what this news is," Constance said, and they moved within the cabin area.

Chapter Nineteen

MATTEO NOTED that the vehicle stopped right outside the gate, and he waited impatiently in the gloom to see what exactly they were after.

Nothing good comes from inviting the enemy inside your camp.

"What's going on, Matteo? Why is there only one vehicle?" James' query filled the air.

He didn't know, so he shook his head.

The door opened and a man emerged. "I'm seeking Matteo Bonita. I wish to discuss matters with him."

"I'm Matteo Bonita. Who are you?" he called back, ensuring his position was shielded from view.

The man wasn't big or even threatening, but Matteo knew looks could be deceiving, particularly in such fraught circumstances. "Vincent Druesling. I'm here on behalf of the castaways of Casa Bonita. We wish to talk. May we enter—"

"Who else is with you?" questioned Matteo, squinting.

"My wife, our guard, our driver. There are four of us. However, my wife... She's unable to walk large distances, hence we'd need to enter in our vehicle." The man waited, and Matteo's brain worked quickly.

He turned to James. "Take ten men, the biggest and burliest. Check the vehicle. Confiscate all weaponry."

James paled. "But what if there's a weapon hidden...?"

"Clearly, they came here, just four people. If they wanted to damage us—unless there is a bomb hidden, and I doubt they'd come if they had that on board—they would have chosen another method, more people." Matteo shrugged. "If we can end this before it escalates..."

"Fine," James muttered, but was clearly unimpressed by the instruction.

Matteo turned away. "I will send some men out. They will inspect your vehicle. Your driver will walk in and one of my people will take control of the vehicle." He wasn't sure they'd accept that, but he needed to drive home that they—he and his people—had the homeport advantage and would exert any and all pressure to ensure their safety.

The man agreed with a firm nod of his head. "We'll await your men." Then he rested his hip against the vehicle and settled in to wait.

Matteo also waited and watched the gates once they opened. His men trooped out and scattered like ants around the vehicle, and with a start, Matteo noted James had gone with them and was now talking animatedly with Vincent.

"Does he know them, Matteo?" the man beside him queried.

Matteo grunted, "I don't know. But it does look that way."

Finally, the vehicle engine started with a whine, and it rolled through the gates, which were then firmly closed.

Hurrying back down the ladder, Matteo allowed scenarios to play through his mind. *Is this a trap? Are they possible allies?* But when he reached the vehicle and opened the car door, his brain ceased working.

"Matteo?" The woman inside the vehicle reached out. His guts twisted.

"Nadia?"

She inclined her head slowly. "Yes, it's me, Matteo. Vincent saved me. I'd been... They all thought I was dead, and to be honest, if Vincent hadn't saved me then, I would have died."

"But I saw you. You were..." Words failed him.

"They cast me into the ocean. Vincent was ready for me because we were lovers. He was... May we take this inside? There's much to tell you, but the time is short, my love. Please?" She smiled and spoke softly, but still his hackles rose.

Matteo shook his head. "I... Come in," he said and gestured for them to enter the building which housed his accommodation. He watched with amazement as she propelled herself out of the vehicle, though slowly and with much grimacing.

"It's not a pretty sight," she laughed. "But I'm alive, and I'm truly happy with Vincent."

He gulped as she propelled herself forward on sticks. "There was gunfire in the town," he blurted out.

"Yes, one of the people in the building got a little excited. I left our men to try to round them up, but they ran away before we could explain we came in peace."

"Was anyone injured?" He needed to know if Constance had survived, and he fisted a hand in his pocket as he waited for Nadia's reply.

"Oh, no one that we could ascertain. And I wouldn't be surprised if whoever was in town and in charge of the residents headed for the dirigibles at the edge of town. Do you know who they are?" She glanced at him then the surroundings once they'd crossed the threshold.

He considered for a moment, then nodded. "Yes. Damien Whitmore, his daughter Constance, and her personal guard."

Nadia's face shifted, and surprise and concern replaced the tight-edged smile she'd sent in his direction. "Oh... Well! We need his support too. I don't suppose..." She looked back, and Matteo noted the soft way her gaze fell on Vincent. "Do you know how to contact them?"

"They were supposed to inspect the building, and I would imagine in the situation would have made for the dirigible, but..."

She winced. "We arrived looking like an army?"

"More an advance party, Nadia."

She sighed. "We need to make contact with them. Would you..."

He turned to James. "Hail the Phoenix. See if there's any contact. We need Damien and Constance here now."

Entering the compound was anti-climactic, thought Constance. They'd been running on adrenaline for the entire afternoon, and now, to learn that their response was too extreme had her wondering how the failure of communications had brought them all to this?

Matteo waited by the door as Constance, Damien, and Anderton arrived, his eyes hooded. The men who'd come with the woman waited outside. Constance had the impression that they weren't so much barred as uncertain, though it was clear the woman was in charge.

"Who?" Constance asked. "Who is she?"

James crowded in. "His sister, Matteo's. Or half-sister. They share a father, and he was close to her, before she was given up for marriage."

Constance's mouth dropped open. *Sister?* Realisation impinged. This was the sister he'd spoken of. The one who'd died. Yet here she was. Alive, if somewhat damaged, judging by the use of her walking stick and her obvious limp.

She was obviously intending to call on that relationship. Something about the situation was off. Wrong. Then Constance shrugged. What would she know? Besides, she was so exhausted after today's experience that she wasn't sure she was thinking clearly. Matteo took her hand, squeezed it, and the ball of ice in her chest melted.

They walked into the dining room, where the ones Matteo called Vincent and Nadia waited. When Nadia was introduced, Constance glanced at Matteo as memories of him telling her that his sister had died impinged.

"Hello, Constance. Mr Whitmore," Nadia said.

"Damien," her father corrected.

"Of course. So, Matteo, what do you need me to explain?" She sat in the chair Constance had come to consider her own, and that set her teeth on edge.

"What's happening? Why did you come here, and how did you survive?" Matteo settled himself in his chair, and Constance and Damien remained by the door.

"Well, as I explained earlier, my husband wasn't what you'd call bright. He thought I was dead, and the child too. It didn't survive." She sighed. "But I lived, and Vincent knew, thanks to my maid keeping him updated. Anyway, they 'consigned' my body to the depths as is Casa

Bonita custom and practice, and Vincent fished me out. He got me the medical care I needed. That's the story of how I survived. As to the other? Our brother, Javier, has indeed been injured, and he and his wife of repute were taken aboard the ship, but his others, those who have power? They're still there and facilitating Javier's plan."

"And that plan is?" Matteo asked.

"We're not totally sure, but I think it's something to do with Lores. He still has Maria, and she's worse than ever. Grotesque, and I'm not sure she's not gone mad. So, we need you to come back and help us." Nadia gazed across the table at him. "They can fill the gaps, I have no doubt." She waved at James, Constance, Damien, and Anderton.

Constance had to fight to hold herself still. If he...

"Nadia, I have responsibilities here—"

She shook her head at Matteo. "But you have staff, Matteo. That's what you trained them for, I would think?" She turned to look at them waiting by the door, smiling as if she couldn't read the tone of the room. "Mr Whitmore? We'll also be looking for assistance with armaments. I know you're doing work for Bloom and his men, so you'd be able to include us in..."

Damien tensed beside Constance. "I only deal with Bloom and those he specifically sent to me."

Nadia's face hardened. "Really? This is a travesty! We're here, looking to free Casa Bonita. Our home, Matteo. Our home. The people who raised us, parented us, are there, in dire straits. They need us, and we owe them!"

Matteo grimaced, and Constance wondered what was going on in his mind. "Nadia, I can't just drop everything. There are hundreds relying on me. They need me and... And I owe them too. Don't ask me to abrogate my response—"

"Rubbish," Nadia bellowed, her cheeks red and eyes bright. "You don't owe them anything near what we should be giving to our own people. Not one bit of what you're saying holds weight."

"Why did you come here, Nadia? You say it's to gain my assistance, but right now all I'm seeing is hate and anger. So, what is it? What do you want?"

She laughed, but the sound chilled Constance's marrow. "I deserve what you have. I deserve a place where I belong. I deserve the financial resources you've been given."

Matteo's laugh was frigid. "What I have I earned. You don't know what I did or how I did without. You've no idea, and what I have is what I've worked damned hard for. No one gave me anything." He punctuated the points with a bang of his fist. "Don't try to tell me what I owe anyone."

Her lips flattened, and Constance watched the icy cold shards of hate settle in her eyes. "Then I have to take what you have." She surged up, pulled out an actinic gun, and fired across the table. "I will take what I want," she muttered as Matteo slumped.

"Matteo!" screamed Constance, rushing forward. She didn't stop because something inside her tore. Was he dead? Her brain felt disconnected from the rest of her body as she simply reacted.

He groaned, and she patted his chest, and realisation dawned. The material he wore, the cut... He was wearing the ballistafabric suit. The one she'd made for him.

James surged forward as Damien and Anderton moved to tackle Nadia. The men who'd travelled with her stood stock-still as if they too were surprised by her actions, and Anderton scooped up the pistol which she'd dropped to the tabletop.

"Matteo? Open your eyes," Constance muttered.

Nadia screeched, "He's dead, you fool! I killed him!"

Matteo's eyes fluttered open. "Shut up, Nadia. I'm not dead, though my chest hurts like I should be."

"How?" she bellowed, roaring her fury.

Constance grabbed Matteo's hand and whirled to face his sister. "The suit. I made it for him, and it absorbed the shot. Your actions failed, Nadia. Now, you'll face Bloom and trial for your actions."

Matteo moved, and Constance assisted him to rise. "Thank you," he muttered to her, and she released him.

He wobbled a little but waved away any further assistance, and though she wanted to help, she understood he needed to stand on his own.

"I wanted to believe you, Nadia," he said. "But something about the way you entered town, the cavalier disregard for everyone else, alerted me that something was wrong. The Nadia I knew would never have acted like this." He paused, rubbed his chest. "The Nadia I knew would understand my people are important to me, and I will attend to their needs first. What I've built is important, not just to me, but to them. I won't relinquish what I have just because you demand it."

He shook his head, the action slow and pained.

"I would have helped you," he continued. "I was ready to assist in any way I could, but this?" He waved to the room, and Constance knew it was more than that. "This is not how you seek assistance from someone."

He slid back down into the seat, and though his colour was returning slowly, Constance itched to get him water, and to find out how to alleviate his current discomfort. Instead, she waited, understanding he wouldn't want to let her know he was weakened, even if temporarily.

"Anderton, round up Nadia's people. Take men and see what you can learn. Damien, would you assist please?" His voice rasped, but the two men audibly assented and left the room. "Nadia, James is going to take you into custody, have you transferred to Bloom, and he will make a recommendation for what happens to you." He coughed, cleared his throat. "James? Please? You'll find restraints in the drawer behind her."

Constance hovered while James restrained Matteo's sister then carried her from the room, not that she went quietly. Feet kicking and screaming, she squirmed and yelled. Constance waited until she was gone from the room.

"Damn it, Matteo, we need to get that off you," she said and began unfastening the buttons and clips that kept his jacket closed.

"Leave it for now," he said. "Come sit beside me."

She frowned. "You need to get comfortable and—"

"Damn it, Constance. Would you sit down, please?" A wealth of frustration threaded his voice. "Please?"

Chapter Twenty

MATTEO'S CHEST ached and his head pounded. It had taken everything to keep upright when dealing with Nadia. The sense of hurt radiated through his chest too, so it was difficult to understand what was physical versus emotional pain. He'd found his sister only to lose her again immediately. He really didn't want to quantify her actions as megalomania, but the word hovered at the edge of his consciousness.

Constance remained close, and it made him feel strangely thankful.

"What did you want to talk about?" She raised a brow, and he wondered if she realised just how beautiful she really was.

"My sister. Nadia is as broken as all of us. Our father, he had much to answer for, and I wanted to give her the benefit of the doubt." He steepled his hands. "I invited her in, not without due thought for the danger."

"But into your home? Your compound? That was a risk to everyone, Matteo." She spoke softly and without heat.

"It was. I hoped for the best but have always been prepared for the worst. Without the suit, I wouldn't have put myself in this position. She didn't know about it, so I could hedge my bets."

"You didn't have the helmet on, Matteo. What if she'd chosen a head-shot?"

He smiled. "One thing I remember, she hates the sight of blood. Makes her nauseous. At close range, there was no chance of that."

"Matteo," she growled.

"Look, I know," he huffed, "I knew Nadia," he amended. "Yes, there would have been blood, but brains spatter." He shuddered, remembering the time he'd seen that first-hand.

"Great, but you need to get that suit off. You need to have a drink of water and get in bed."

He winked at Constance. "With you?"

She threw up her hands. "Really? You're going to flirt with me right now?"

He smiled, because she'd taken on a rosy glow, and it lightened her concerns. "Well, there's no one else I'd rather flirt with."

"Matteo..."

A knock came at the door. "Come in," he called.

James entered the room. "Damien is going to take Nadia on the Phoenix. He'll return in the morning, and our men have her husband, driver, and guard in hand. They're going to round up the others, interrogate them. Damien is leaving his own guards for now for our safety, and once we know the situation, he's suggested Bloom's men should take control, ensure they're tried in a court." James shifted. "I'd like to go with him. I think, having one of our own there, we can answer any questions Bloom has, and will add gravitas to his argument."

Matteo considered the suggestion. "That sounds like it's workable. When does he plan to leave?"

"Within the hour. Damien said we can travel through the night, the distance is only about eight hours, so we can get there, deliver the prisoner, meet with Bloom, and return before sunset tomorrow," James explained.

Matteo nodded and his friend left the room. "Tell me what happened," he said to Constance.

"You were shot," she answered with a grin. "That was probably the big thing that occurred today."

His fingers burrowed through his hair, and a burst of pain stole his breath. He saw stars, and it took a moment, and more than a few blinks, to clear his mind. "That wasn't what I meant. Today. Where were you?"

Constance sighed, rubbed her forehead, then gazed at him. "We were in the mercantile building, inspecting it, when people started streaming past."

Now she rubbed her eyes, and he could see her exhaustion. He would have preferred to tell her it was all okay, that she could rest, but he needed to know what had taken place.

"Anderton and Damien, along with myself, got them inside. We battened down, not being sure what would occur." Her smile was thin, little more than a flattening of her lips. "One of the men, civilians, shot, and that caused issues which alerted Nadia's people that we were holed up in the building, because we were sure no one knew. Then I was on the roof and a brick fell."

Constance shrugged, but he didn't miss the wince which told him there was more to the story than she was sharing.

"Anyway," she continued, "we left after Damien gave instructions to the civilians. Women and children were to gather near the larger dirigible immediately after dark. They scattered to take shelter out of sight, and we hid in shadows until nearly dusk, got ourselves to the side of the dock, and alerted the crew of the Phoenix, then got on board." She shrugged again. "You know what happened after that."

He reached out, grabbed her hand. "I heard you earlier. Talking to Damien."

She stiffened and hissed in a breath. "That was nothing to do with you."

Fury scoured him, but he didn't want secrets between them. Not now. His fears during the last few hours had crystallised a truth he hadn't wanted to admit. His feelings were deeper than lust. The terror that had ridden him all day... He shook his head.

"I... I was worried about you." He grimaced. "More than worried, and James had to talk me out of coming for you."

"Why? Because you feel pity? Poor little girl with a horrible backstory? She's broken, and what? You plan to fix me?" Her lips trembled.

"No, Constance. Because you're the strongest woman I know. Nadia? She had someone to lean on. You leaned on yourself. You took the opportunities presented and made yourself into someone. That's..."

He felt small and stupid. He wanted to tell her but was second-guessing himself. "I... I care, Constance."

Her eyes widened. "What?"

"I'm tangled inside, Constance. Caring for someone is like being slammed with a sledgehammer. It takes a lot for me to look outside myself, and I'm..." How the hell do I get the words out?

She rose, took his hand. "I think you hit your head when she shot you. Bed is where you should be." Her words were curt, almost surly, and he let her assist him to rise, to pull him to the bedroom. Waited quietly as she unfastened the suit, and he relinquished the clothing like a child, all the while watching her.

Seeing the hints that she cared too.

When he was stripped down to his underwear, she laid his suit over the chair. "Goodnight, Matteo," she whispered, but he grabbed her hands. Didn't let her go.

"Stay. Stay with me tonight," he muttered. "Let me hold you." She turned stiff again, and he cursed himself, because he'd heard her words, the truth that the nightmares still visited her. "Not because of that," he explained. "Because I need you here. With me."

Seconds passed, long and heavy, then she slumped against him. "All right."

"I'm not happy about you listening to a private conversation," Constance told Matteo as they lay side by side on the bed.

"I didn't mean to. At least, not initially," he explained. "But as you started to speak, I felt... I know you didn't want me to know, but would you have told me? At some point in the future if our connection continued?"

She considered his question. "I don't know," Constance whispered. And she really didn't. After all, he'd learned about the thing that tore at her, night after night. About the secrets she'd kept for over a decade. Hearing someone else knew about your weakness... well, that was terrifying. Because once they understood what you feared most, they could use that.

But what if he didn't?

That question haunted her too. Because if she let down her guard, how would he act? They'd already clashed—more than once—but none of them were deep. Not like learning about her greatest secrets.

"Constance, I was terrified you'd be hurt today."

She turned to face him. "Why?"

"Because I care about you. I couldn't reach you. I don't like not being in control, and you were beyond my reach."

She considered his words, glanced at his face, searching for a hint of the story behind them. All she read was sincerity and remembered fear. "I'm sorry you were concerned. Damien protected me, but I'm more than capable of looking after myself. He taught me well."

He was contemplating her words; she could read that on his face too. "While I'm pleased he did, the fact that you need to... I want to ensure your safety, and the whole situation felt unnatural."

She cupped his cheek. "Everything about the houses is unnatural. It's taught you that women must be submissive and weak. We're not. I'm not, Matteo."

He nodded. "You're right."

Caressing his cheek, she leaned in and kissed him softly on the lips. "You should sleep. You'll feel better in the morning."

Time passed, and she stayed close, wishing she could hold him. *If only*, the two words that summed up her life. She squeezed her eyes shut, let the energy burst she'd felt at thinking she'd lost him drain away, and as she was drifting to sleep, she was sure he whispered, "I love you, Constance."

She slept, and Matteo lay still, hearing the whisper of her breath. Why had he told her that? The words he'd never uttered to another living soul had slid out. It was as if they had a mind of their own.

But it was done, and in hindsight, he didn't regret them. They were true. Today had been the longest day of his life, the fear spiking through him, and he never wanted to experience that again. He'd do whatever it took to protect her.

Grey swam at the edges of consciousness, and sleep tugged him below its surface.

Constance woke with a jerk. Matteo had obviously risen while she'd slept, and she cursed the need to make sure he was well and recovered.

Yet, there was work to do. Things to order for the mercantile and James' suit to complete. She also had to begin the process of outfitting his men, finding out which women had sewing skills and testing them to see just how much they knew and who'd be a fit for her new endeavour.

"So much to do, and so little time," she muttered and rose, her hands lifting to her hair. Catching sight of herself in the mirror, she noted her wild state.

She'd just set about arranging her tresses when the door opened, and she turned. Matteo strode into the room. "I was coming to see if you'd risen yet." In his hands there was a steaming cup, and Constance smiled and slid the last pin into her hair.

"I hope that's coffee? I never got used to the hot chocolate or cups of tea in London."

Matteo's smile widened. "It's coffee. You can have it here or in the dining room?"

"Dining room, I think. I have some things I want to run past you, then I need to get to the workroom."

He held the door wide, and she brushed past him, a smile on her face. *I could get very used to this.*

Then the smile melted off her face. After all, he'd promised her nothing except for what they had now. She watched as he placed the cup on the table. "Breakfast will be served in a few minutes. Now, what did you want to ask me or tell me?"

Constance settled in her chair, and for a second, she saw a flash of yesterday's incident and that gave her momentary pause. "I... I wanted to know if any of the women here know how to sew. Or may be looking to learn a skill that would give them a chance of employment."

Matteo frowned. "I don't know. Until now, the main concern has been how to keep everyone safe, but there is a town hall session later today. If you'd like to speak then, you can ask them directly."

"Oh. Well, that would work very well. I'll also be looking for someone with book-keeping skills, a floor manager, and someone to take control of my store." She ticked off the positions on her hand.

"So, you plan to stay then?" he asked, and she got the impression he was pleased by what she was suggesting.

"Yes. Damien and I agreed the mercantile building is a perfect fit for my needs. I will need some tradesmen to prepare the building, but that can be taking place while I train staff."

"And you'll live where?"

"There's a space upstairs that, with a little work, will be perfect. I won't need staff for the house immediately, as I'm a confident cook, and some services I think are already available in town, such as a laundry, yes?"

Matteo nodded. "When?"

"Well, if I can get the transfer completed in the next few days, I can make enquiries for builders..."

"I know we have a few on-site. I'll talk to them if you'd like?"

Constance bit her lip. "I'd rather..." But what would she ask? "I'll draw you a plan of what I'd like. If you could have them prepare me a quote—"

"There's no need, Constance. We can..."

She shook her head. "No. This is business." His easy smile nearly disarmed her, but she was determined. "I need to do this properly."

"Fine. However, remember, you'll be working for me. Outfitting my men and—"

She laughed. "Yes, but that's working for my father. However, the inside workings of my building are different. So, normal rates, Matteo. I have the resources."

His smile died away, and she wondered why. "Fine. I'll have the men look at the building, and we'll present you with a quotation for the works tomorrow. Then, if you're satisfied, we'll make arrangements for the work to begin. I doubt what you need will take long. There are enough men to complete the work in quick order, given many of them were trained building these shelters, sheds, and even reinforcing the walls of the compound."

A sound heralded the delivery of breakfast, so she nodded. "Thank you, Matteo."

Once the food was delivered, they ate in silence.

Chapter Twenty-One

JAMES RETURNED THAT EVENING, and Matteo was pleased to see him. Without his right-hand man, it felt like he was hobbled in completing the tasks he normally took for granted. "Good, now we have a few tasks I need completed this evening. We held a town hall meeting earlier today," Matteo explained, and James frowned.

"Without me?"

"Things are moving at a rapid pace, James. How did you get on with Bloom?"

James shook his head. "Damien is... forceful. I barely got a word in, but Nadia has been delivered, and Anderton is arranging the delivery of her husband, guard, and the head of their security detail." A moment passed. "I think the plan is to keep them separated so they can't conspire. Nadia and her husband, I mean."

"Good, then we can focus on preparing the men. Constance has your suit almost completed, and she's busy in her workroom. You should go see her soon, have your final fitting. She has a list of the men she wishes to see tomorrow to begin the process of cutting out their suits."

James peered into the living room. "She's not here?"

Matteo shook his head. "No. She's interviewing women right now and setting tasks for those who have indicated they have sewing experience to hire for her business. She's purchasing the mercantile building and will employ women, after she's checked their skill levels and trained them as necessary."

"To make the suits?" James' query was soft.

"What? Oh no. I'm not sure she's willing to relinquish that to women who are unskilled. No, this is to make bespoke gowns and items suitable for mail-order. She's looking to skill the women so her products are of a quality that women will continue to come back for more, as she explained it."

"I see." James poured himself a drink from the decanter. "And you're comfortable with her taking on a role like that? In business?"

Matteo grunted. "She's a strong and independent woman, James. I don't have the right to ask her not to."

"But you have feelings for her. You have intentions?"

Matteo sighed. "I can't ask that of a woman like her. Not while my hands are tied with Casa Bonita."

"You haven't considered giving that up? Not for Constance?"

Matteo glanced at his friend. "No. The men and women who are prisoners of the blasted house deserve their freedom. To be able to make their own decisions and to…"

James quirked his eyebrow. "What?"

"If they are free, then so will I be. Women like Maria and Nadia will no longer have to pay the price. No one deserves to be a prisoner like that."

James sipped his drink, and Matteo wondered what his friend was thinking. "What about Lores?"

"What about him? If he's taken into custody and handed over to Bloom…" Matteo shrugged. "Once the hive is destroyed, then we can begin the process of reintegrating the residents into society."

James grunted. "I'm going in to see Constance. I'll see you in the morning."

Matteo watched as the man left the room, but an uneasiness settled like a rock in his belly. He didn't know why or how, but something was off.

Constance nodded to James as he entered the room. "Come on, hop on the stand and I'll finish the fitting. This should be ready later today."

His gaze swept around the room. "This meets with your approval? You have everything you need?"

"Yes. I mean, I must share the room with Matteo, but overall, it's workable," she answered, taking up the chalk and sliding the pincushion onto her wrist.

"And the storage?" He moved from one foot to the other.

"I left most of the fabric on the Phoenix. Only brought two bolts, though that's more than enough. The rest will be delivered to the mercantile once it's completed. My father is planning for the works to be completed with Matteo and is arranging for security measures to be included," she murmured as she pinned the hems. "Turn please," she instructed, and he did.

"What kind of measures?" James' voice sounded distracted.

"What? Oh, I don't know. That's not something I have any experience with."

"And the guards?"

"I think he's got particular ideas and is pulling them in from Raphael—my sister's husband—from his estate and from Nobel Crest. He's been training men there for the last few years. They're exceptional, according to Damien. The best force available."

James grunted, and she started to mark the fit for the buttons. "You prefer suspenders?"

"I... Yes. And for the jacket to have a high neck. Oh, and one of those masks that Matteo has."

She sighed. "Sorry, can't do that. They require a lot of hours, and a great deal of fitting. I gave mine to Matteo, and that took me weeks to create."

Constance stepped back.

"Now then, let's try the jacket, shall we?" She slid it over his shoulder and frowned at the way the back sat. "How did that happen?" She made a mental note to unpick the back seam, and to taper it just a little more.

"I'm done?" Once again James hopped from foot to foot.

"Yes. I should have it ready probably tomorrow morning."

"Fine. Ah, maybe you'd give me a tour of the mercantile then too?"

She smiled. "Perhaps. Now, if you change out of those pants, I'll get started."

"Of course." He stepped down from the stand. "Do you miss living in one of the houses?" he asked before shaking his head. "Of course not. I don't know what came over me." He moved behind the screen she'd had set up, and while his comment left her frowning, she didn't really think any more of it.

He left the room, and she scooped up the pants, ready to begin. "I need to unpick that seam. Look at tapering just a little more. Then I can reshape it." She settled into the chair and set to work.

Chapter Twenty-Two

MATTEO SWIPED the perspiration from his forehead. "You're sure about that?"

Anderton nodded. "The informant is as good as his word."

"Where is she then?" he demanded of the man opposite him.

"In the office, working on James' suit. I've someone watching her currently. She's not going to be left alone."

The papers in his hands, proof that there was a mole in their midst, curdled the contents of his stomach. He re-read the words, committing them to memory.

Once I have a chance, I'll take her hostage. He'll do anything now. He's emotionally committed to the woman. Fancy that! Matteo Bonita has a woman he's chosen. Not that I believe it to be something he'll act on.

I won't take any chances. You taught me well. I just must find a way to set it up without him knowing. Then I'll strike. The other men, the ones who will support me, know I'm ready to strike. I just need to make sure no one finds out who I am.

"And you've no idea, Anderton?" he demanded, gaze roaming the bodies moving within the compound. No one had left yet. Maybe he should let them go, so he had less to worry about? Would that assist or make the situation worse?

"No. It was found hidden in the ceiling of the bunkroom. But since all the men use that space, and the rooms are each filled with six to eight bunks, it's impossible to work out who it might be."

Matteo scrunched his eyes. "You're right." And he needed to tread carefully, because he needed the men to see him as a leader, not someone blindly stumbling from one threat to the next. He was loathe to raise it outside of the three of them—Damien, Anderton, and himself.

And James? He could tell him, but it wasn't his security at risk, it was Constance's. Anderton had been firm in bringing the book to his attention. Damien had instructed him not to share it with anyone else.

"She trusts you, you know," Anderton said, and the words startled him. "I travelled with her to London. It's why Damien sent me again this time. She's not one who quickly trusts anyone. After Francesca and Raphael, Damien trained several of us. I was chosen as Constance's guard because my skills were complementary, according to Damien. He felt I could fill the holes in her ability to say safe. Someone she could talk to in her weak moments. She tries hard to hide them. Hell, I don't think even Damien understands just how fragile she is. She's like... She's like a little sister to me. But you, she trusted you quickly. I've never seen her like that in all the years I've known her."

"What exactly do you mean?" Matteo swung to face the man.

"I mean, you could hurt her. You already have." Anderton's gaze zeroed right through him. "She's special, Matteo, but soft too."

"I have no intention of hurting her. Not ever again." He rubbed a hand over his chest. "I... I don't know what I can offer her."

Anderton laughed. "Only you can work that out, but I'd advise you to find some speed about it. But until you do, protect her." He sighed. "I don't do mushy, feminine chatter, so I'll leave it at that. By the way, Damien expects a question from you soon. He's instructed me to tell you to get your wits about you, because other men know she's back." He smiled, and Matteo stared at Anderton as he walked away.

"A question?" *Could he mean...?* Surely Damien hadn't realised that they'd been intimate?

He sighed. Just another conundrum to consider once this damned mess was sorted.

James entered the courtyard where Matteo had met with Anderton. "I was looking for you," he muttered.

"Your last fitting?"

James grunted. "Constance said she thought the suit would be ready tomorrow. I wonder, would it be worth looking at the mercantile building? I know she said Damien had the planning for security underway, but since she's going to be so near, perhaps it would be wise if we looked and suggested an evacuation point? Something where she and ourselves know where she'd emerge in a dangerous situation?"

Matteo stared at his friend. "You think that will be necessary?"

"Nadia isn't the only sibling you have, and with Maria's enhancement, it's not clear if they would use her. I think any plan where you're ahead in the game would be worthwhile."

Matteo considered James' words. Together with the knowledge Anderton had brought to him, perhaps James was right. If they prepared, they'd be in a better position to survive another attack. "Yes, but how soon...?"

"You're sending the citizens home tomorrow? How about then. We'd be less noticeable. I could take her in the automotive and be there and back in little time."

"I'm not sure Anderton will let you drive the machine," Matteo said with a laugh.

"I think you can find something to keep him busy." The other man laughed and retreated, leaving Matteo considering the request.

Constance felt strangely alone. She'd only been here days, but in that time, she'd spent most of her nights with Matteo. Tonight, he'd seemed distant, so she'd kept herself occupied until fatigue was overwhelming.

Retiring to the bedroom, she dragged on a soft lawn nightgown and settled in the bed, journal on her lap.

I've done something exceptionally stupid. I've fallen in love with a man who is beyond my reach.
The nights with him have been inexplicable. I've felt whole, and yet, I've never felt more lonely than I do now. How can that be?
The knowledge that when I leave the compound I'll be embarking on a long and lonely life fills me with grief, but there's no hope for anything else. He's committed to the destruction of Casa Bonita, and I would be a distraction he can't afford. I need him to succeed, and I'll do everything I can, yet the prospect of years of watching him…

A teardrop marred her last words, and she swiped another from her cheek. The future would be grim unless she looked forward, considering what she could do for others.

The mercantile is my future. I will be the aunt to my siblings' children. I am committed to helping others provide a future for themselves and their families, to make a life and build hope for a brighter future. It will be enough. I will make a difference. I will be content with that. I must be.

Constance sighed, blew on the words to dry the ink, then closed the book. Long ago she'd learned that she was far too broken for others to see her as a future partner. She had no illusions.

"Goodnight," she whispered into the silence and lay back, closing her eyes.

Returning from his office, Matteo frowned at the empty room. He checked his bedroom next, but it too was empty.

Then he heard the first sound of distress coming from Constance's room. He opened the door, and she lay in the bed, face pale in the moonlight, hair damp against her cheek as she twisted and turned. "No…" she muttered. "Don't do that." The words tore at him because he knew what lay behind them.

He settled a hip on the bed, laid a hand on her shoulder, and she shied away, memories no doubt dictating her actions. "Constance, it's okay. It's Matteo. Wake up," he whispered, every whimper a dagger in his chest.

"Ma... Matteo? What?" Her eyes opened.

He dragged her close, felt the dampness of her gown. "You were having a nightmare, love." The rapid beat of her heart and the chill of her skin told him that for all she was keeping her defences up, they were insubstantial. "I couldn't... I couldn't just leave you alone, sweetheart."

Her fingers gripped his jacket. "It was awful, but... I've had this nightmare before," she explained.

"Tell me about it, Constance. We can defeat it together."

She shook her head. "No. I don't want to talk about it, Matteo. Make love to me. Right now," she demanded. "Make me feel whole."

God knew he wanted to, especially if it would banish the darkness that terrified her night after night. "Don't ask me to do that. What we have..."

Constance tugged away. "You don't want me," she muttered, and he grabbed her hand, thrust it against his groin.

"Not want you? I want you so much I ache for you, all day, every day. But I won't let you use it." He gentled his voice. "We have something special. It's more than anything I could have expected."

"Nonsense," she growled. "When I leave here, we're done."

He jerked back to look at her face. "No. Yes, we can't take the steps I want until I finalise what I've promised. I must take down Casa Bonita. I have people I need to free, but once that's over, I will come for you, Constance."

She laughed discordantly. "No, you won't. What you say now will melt away like snow. What we have is physical but not—"

"No. I mean it when I say I will come for you." But it was obvious that she didn't believe him. Derision screamed from her pursed lips and frown. "Damn it. It's my intention to marry you once I complete my mission. I want children with you. I want a future. I love you, Constance."

Her eyes took on a sheen of tears. "Don't promise me what you can't give me. That's cruel."

He grabbed her shoulders. "I mean it…"

"Then make the promise now, or not at all." She quivered in his grip.

He stopped, considered her words. "You'd take me on now? When nothing is settled? You're willing to take that chance?"

Her mouth opened. "What… you mean marry immediately?"

He nodded. "I'd do anything for you. I told you I'd love you. I wanted to wait, to be free to give you everything, but if waiting isn't an option, then I'll do that too." He would, because the idea that she might not believe him, or someone else might come in and scoop her up before he could secure her promise wasn't an option.

It wasn't quite the way he'd have thought to propose, but if she needed the reassurance now, he'd give it to her.

"Marry me, Constance. I'll make arrangements, and later, when we can, we can have a second ceremony so your family can attend if you want."

His heart beat fast while he waited for her response.

Seconds passed. Long seconds.

"I never thought this would happen for me. I…" She licked her lips, and his eyes followed the movement, his body hardening.

"Yes. Say it." Any other response would destroy him. She hadn't said the words he suddenly needed like lungs needed air, but there'd be time. Years. One day, she'd let go of the last bind which contained the woman she hid from everyone else. One day. He could afford to give her that.

"Yes," she whispered, but he didn't miss the fear in her eyes.

"I'll make you happy, Constance. I promise." He sealed the words with a kiss. It was soft, and though he wanted more, tonight he kept the caress chaste. "Thank you," he said, before resting his forehead against hers.

Constance woke, the bed soft, the arms around her warm.

He'd asked and she'd assented last night. It was fuzzy around the edges, but she remembered well enough the conversation.

Marriage.

She'd told herself that would never be. She hadn't looked for a suitor in London, believing, clearly mistakenly, that this would never come to pass. She knew Ammy had lined up several possible suitors, and she'd thought that once she explained to her that she was staying in Bald Head, they'd be sent her way. She'd have time and strength to send them away.

Instead, this man, the one in the bed beside her, would be her husband.

He'd promised a quick union now, with the froth and bubble of the formal event later. She bit her lip.

"You can't get out of it, Constance." Matteo rolled over and took the hand she'd been unconsciously worrying.

"I'm not..." She shook her head. "It's not that."

"Then tell me, what is worrying you?" He levered up on an elbow.

Where to begin? "I... I told myself I'd never bring a child into the world where there was a chance I'd have to give up control. I saw what that does, and most marriages, those I know of, they're about power. The power the man holds over a woman. I was so hurt by what I saw and experienced that power to me was vital. It's why working alone is the way I like it. I guess it's why when I saw what you were doing here, it just sort of connected for me. I saw the good I could do, giving other women hope and a chance to make a future for themselves, either with a husband or alone." She shrugged. "It sounds like I'm centred in what's right for me, but it gave me a freedom—"

"I'm not going to ask you to give that up, Constance." His hand slid over hers and warmth filled her. "If that's what you feel you need to do, I'll support you. We can move there after Casa Bonita, but I can't do that yet. But what you've proposed, it has merit, my love."

She blinked. "You've never called me that."

"My failure, love. You deserve to be wooed, and..." He shrugged, and she noted the red tide creeping over his cheeks. "I didn't give you that."

"Matteo, I don't need that. Not really. If I'm honest, it was never an expectation I welcomed. I've not been without opportunities, but I didn't want..." *How do I explain that he's enough? That I didn't want the traditional bouquets and carriage rides, picnics, and opera.* "I don't want parties and cakes and *billet doux*. I never did. What you offer? It's someone who will walk beside me. It's honest, and that means more to me than any pretty garlands and half-made promises."

Inhaling, she considered what else it was that he was offering. "I want someone who will give me the space to find out what I can do. Someone who won't demand my attention all day, every day, because he can. Someone who understands I need to be valued, not for how I look or act, but because of who I am. Me."

Listing the reasons he was right for her was a revelation.

Matteo must have seen something on her face, as he leaned in. "What, Constance?"

She dragged in a sudden deeply unsteady breath. "I... I think I love you, Matteo." Terror clawed at her. She was releasing the most sacred of words and emotions to him.

His smile was like a sunrise. Bright. Shining. Warming. He dragged her close, and she felt the slow beat of his heart. "And I love you, Constance. I wasn't ready for it, but when I was sure I'd lose you, it was there. A crystal in the darkness, illuminating the empty places inside me."

"So, now what?" she whispered.

He sighed. "I'd love to seal this with more than a kiss, but we must rise. I need to talk with Damien, make arrangements. Have a wedding. All in a day's work," he growled, and she laughed.

"All in a day's work, huh? Well, I guess we best rise." She rolled but he pulled her back under him and kissed her.

Heat flashed through her, and by the end she was moaning and arching against him. "Damn it," he muttered, and she giggled as he tugged away. "You find this funny?"

"Well, I was going to rise, but you're the one..." she pointed out.

He grunted and she climbed from the bed, looking down at her wrinkled clothing. "I need to change."

When Matteo glanced at her, heat flashed deep inside. "Don't tempt me, love. Be quick. I'll meet you in the dining room."

Then he left her, and she took a moment, raising her fingers to her lips with a smile.

Damien was in the dining room as Matteo emerged from Constance's room. The man watched him. While Matteo wasn't strictly embarrassed —after all, they'd not been doing anything untoward—there was a realisation that Damien knew they were comfortable enough with each other that this wasn't something untoward. Not this time anyway.

"Constance is awake?" Damien queried, and Matteo nodded, taking a seat at his customary place. Head of the table. He wondered if that man realised that right now he needed to reclaim control?

"I wanted to inform you that I asked Constance to marry me last night. She agreed." He cleared his throat because Damien's face broke into a smile. "Don't get too excited just yet. Let me explain how we wish our marriage to occur."

Damien frowned. "How you wish it to occur?"

"Yes. We wish a quick union now, with a celebration at a later point. We won't be making any announcements, just..."

"She's agreed to this?" Damien asked.

"Yes," Matteo answered. "Together, we've made the decision. I was happy to wait, but Constance—"

"Is here behind you. And yes, Father. This is what I want."

Matteo turned to gaze at her. She'd changed into fresh and unrumpled pants and blouse, her hair pulled back into a neat coil. She took the place beside Matteo, grabbed his hand, and deepened the connection by sliding her thumb over his hand.

"Then I will, of course, consent, but your mother—"

"Ammy will understand. Just like you and Francesca, it's just..." She cleared her throat. "I love him."

Damien's face softened, and Matteo sighed. "We will marry this afternoon if it can be arranged. We won't announce anything publicly, but after Casa Bonita is freed, we'll have a celebration. A society wedding if that's what everyone wants." Privately, he couldn't think of anything worse. He'd rather a quiet family event, but if that's what Constance wanted, then it was what she'd get.

"All right, I'll need to communicate this to Ammy and the rest of the family," Damien said, and Constance nodded.

"Tell them not to share outside the family, for now, please," she added, and Damien agreed with an inclination of his head.

Matteo waited in silence, watching the father and daughter discuss how they would proceed. "You'll live where?" asked Damien.

"We'll stay here for now. But later, should we decide to relocate to the mercantile, the initial plans will allow for us to be over the shop, so to speak," Matteo explained. "But of course, we'll discuss that at a later stage."

"All right, however, I think we'll continue with the planning for security for the shop, and I'll leave the automotive here for Constance. You will keep Anderton here for as long as he's happy to remain. Should we need to replace him, then I'll handpick a replacement guard for you. Both of you will require increased security. Bloom contacted me overnight. Things are happening at Casa Bonita, and Nadia knows more than she'd been willing to share. He's sending men out there to reconnoitre."

Suddenly Matteo was totally alert. "Like what?"

"I'm waiting for more information, but my bet would require you to be prepared to travel to Casa Bonita. I'll come with you, seeing as how Constance will be safe here, within the compound with Anderton. We can take the Phoenix," Damien added.

Matteo nodded. "After the wedding though. I made a promise, and I intend to see it through." He smiled at Constance, who continued to grip his fingers.

Damien rose. "I'll make arrangements for the Phoenix. You will let me know—"

Matteo nodded. "I'll send word for the preacher. You will be a witness?"

"Yes," Damien responded then left the room.

Matteo stood. "Do you want breakfast?"

Constance shook her head. "I'll have a coffee then try to get James' suit finished this morning. I, uh... I also want to find clothes, bathe, and..." She bit her lip. "I don't have anything suitable, except one gown."

He was once again delighted with the small blush that coloured her cheeks. "Wear it. We'll have a quiet meal here tonight, then I imagine tomorrow—"

Constance nodded, and he knew she understood what wasn't being said. *Tomorrow I'll leave for Casa Bonita.*

Now that she'd finished James' suit, Constance retreated to her room. The tiny scrap of a note which Matteo had sent spoke volumes in her mind.

The preacher will be here after three. He's willing to marry us.
M

His slashing script reminded her that he was very much a man on a mission. One who knew what he wanted and found ways to ensure he achieved it. She was one of them, wasn't she?

Yet, it wasn't trepidation zinging through her at the thought of their forthcoming union. It was excitement. Pleasure. A sense of coming home.

So, she hurried through her ablutions, washing and drying her hair, and choosing her most delicate undergarments, each decorated with a tiny periwinkle cross stitch. Constance had chosen to include the luscious, rose-scented salts to her water, and she could even now detect the faint floral notes on her skin.

Her gown was a pale, powdery blue, which fitted like a glove, with a tiny bustle to the rear and a form-fitting bodice that displayed her attributes. Her hair was coiled and shone after the brushing it out. Now she waited by the mirror, wondering if it was all a bit too much.

A knock sounded at her door, and she rose, smoothing down the skirt of the gown with shaking fingers. "Come," she called, and Damien entered the room.

"My dear, you look exquisite."

Constance blushed. "Thank you, Father."

"I wanted to spend these last few minutes with you. It is important to me that you're happy. You love him, don't you?" Damien peered intently at her, and she nodded.

"I really do. He's ... He's willing to accept the real me. The one who's not comfortable socially. He doesn't demand my obedience but wants me to do and be what I think I can achieve."

"Then I'm comforted. I contacted Ammy. She's sad she couldn't attend but understands completely. She sends her love and best wishes and says that once you're ready and able, she'd like to have a more formal affair. Francesca and Raphael also send their love, as do the rest of your siblings." Damien brushed away the tears that dripped down her cheeks. "Be happy, sweetheart."

He handed her a handkerchief and waited as she employed it to wipe away the last of the moisture. "I'm ready," she breathed.

Damien took her hand, tucked it into the crook of his elbow, and they made their way into the living area.

Matteo waited, along with a man and a woman she presumed to be his wife. The book in his hands was a giveaway this was the preacher.

Damien gave her hand to Matteo who smiled. "I thought having a woman in attendance would make you feel more comfortable," he whispered into her ear.

She gave a quick nod and what she guessed was a wobbly smile. "Thank you," she whispered, then they both turned to the man waiting for them.

The words she'd never expected to repeat, the promises flowed, as she joined her life to Matteo. He slid a band onto her hand, a promise of a future. She looked at it, a tangible reminder of the never-ending circle of love and commitment, and the knowledge filled her with a quiet joy.

Then it was done, congratulations were extended, paperwork completed.

Damien kissed her on the cheek and shook Matteo's hand and left them.

Just the two of them.

"I've arranged a light meal to be delivered soon." Matteo looked suddenly ill-at-ease.

"What's wrong, Matteo?"

"Nothing, just... You're beautiful, wife. When I first saw you, you captured my attention, standing in the hallway of your father's home." He shook his head. "I'm just a humble fisherman, and somehow, I caught the prize."

She laughed. "Prize? I don't think so. I'm a mere seamstress."

"No." Matteo shook his head. "You're a marvel. The woman who learned of the ballistafabric and designed a suit to assist in battle. The woman who could live in comfort yet made the decision to help others. My wife."

She blinked. "My husband." She reached for his hand. "Mine." She dragged him closer and kissed him on the lips. "I rather like doing that," she whispered.

"So do I," he muttered and dove in again.

A knock sounded, and she squeezed her eyes shut as Matteo looked over her shoulder. "On the table. Thank you, Sarah." At his words, she opened her eyes and glanced over her shoulder to watch as the girl slid the tray onto the surface and left.

"There'll be chatter," Constance murmured.

"Let them chatter. We're married, so this is more than acceptable."

She laughed. "Perhaps, but maybe we should lock the door, so no one else can enter and surprise us?"

"Good thinking, my love." He released her and moved to the door. The lock snicked shut, then he turned back, grinned. "Our privacy is assured."

She shook her head. "The door to the office too." As he moved, she stepped to the windows and shut the curtains so all that illuminated them was the light of the lamp.

Matteo turned. "Would you like to eat?"

Constance smiled, a tiny lifting of her lips. "No." Holding out her hand, she waited for him to understand the need building inside her.

"Then come, my wife." He took her hand and led her to the bedroom. His bedroom. *Their bedroom.*

Silence wound around them, a ribbon filled with unspoken longing. Once within the room, she let go, moved to the small bedside table and the lamp. Her fingers found the switch and the flickering glow illuminated the room.

Their gazes met, meshed, and she reached for the buttons at her back.

"Let me," he breathed and brushed away her fingers.

He moved slowly, taking care as he released the pearls then kissed the flesh beneath as he exposed it.

Her hand rested on her belly as the heat of his breath danced fire over her skin. The only sound that wreathed them was her breath and his.

Heat started licking at her, demanding more, as her breasts firmed and ached, heavy with sensual need. Her eyes slid shut, and she moaned as the gown released her, sliding to the floor with a hiss.

His hands surrounded her waist, propelled her back against him, and she couldn't miss the jut of his arousal. "You're delectable," he said. "Like a dainty treat served, meant to be savoured."

Her inhalation was wobbly as his hands slid upward over the layers of chemise and petticoat, corset, and pantalets. Even through the layers of fabric she felt the scorching burn of his touch, and she arched, needing more. The heat between her legs melting as hunger rose.

His lips found the curve of her neck, and she moaned, wanting more. His touch roamed her body, finding the ties and undoing them with unsteady movements.

"Let me help," she whispered.

"This is my pleasure," he murmured against her ear, while propelling her toward the door. "Look," he urged, and she gasped as she noted him in the mirror hanging on the door. Her face flushed, eyes bright and lips swollen. His hands toyed with the petticoat, then it fell, followed by her pantalets.

From the waist down she was naked. She squirmed slightly, noting how his hand was sliding over her skin, to find her most intimate place, then delved between her legs.

"Look at me touching you," he said.

"Matteo," she pleaded, because the arousal within her demanded them both bare. Now. "Please..."

"Please what, my love? Please touch you like this?" He parted her legs enough that his hand could squirm against her sensitive flesh. "Or this?" His other hand covered her still-clad breast, gently massaging it. "Or this?" The timbre of his voice changed as he leaned in to kiss her.

Scorching her.

When it was done, she could barely stand. "Clothes... off," she muttered.

He laughed. "Your wish is my command, wife."

Matteo's clothes hit the floor and he stared at the image of the two of them, naked, mirrored back at them. His darker skin against her pale, creamy flesh. She'd removed the last of her coverings, and his gaze roamed her body. It was as if he was seeing her for the first time.

His hands covered her breasts, peaked nipples jutting against his palms. "You are luscious, my love. You have the body of a goddess, perfectly designed for love, yet your mind is sharp." His hands roamed down her body, finding her belly. "One day, this will be full of our child."

Her breath came in a gasp. "Matteo..."

His fingers dipped lower. "And here, you're full of fire. Heat that makes me want you more and more. Welcoming me home."

He slid a finger inside her, and she moaned and arched, and his body ached to possess her. "Come for me, my love. I want to see the fire on your skin, the flash in your eyes."

And she moved, hips rhythmically rolling for him until she cried out.

He scooped her up, carried her to the bed, laid her down, and prepared to slide within her. "I love you, Constance. I always will." He slid home, and it felt like heaven.

Chapter Twenty-Three

CONSTANCE WOKE TO AN EMPTY SPACE, his pillow cold and a note lying there for her.

My dearest Constance,
I didn't want to wake you, so didn't have a chance to say goodbye.
Damien and I have left aboard the Phoenix to survey the damage
at Casa Bonita. He's left guards adequate to keep you safe, but I
will add my reminder, please stay safe. Only travel out with
Anderton, and make sure to leave notice of where you go and when
you'll likely be back. I'll return as soon as I can.
Take care, my love.
Matteo

Her fingers traced and retraced the 'my love' on the page. Wed less than twenty-four hours and already he'd left her to attend to duty. She couldn't claim she was unaware of his plans, though the ache in her chest reminded her that she still wished it wasn't so.

"Stay safe, Matteo," she muttered, hoping the universe would hear and protect him.

She rose and bathed, dressed hastily, and with a quick thought, slid the ring off her hand and onto a chain around her neck. "Too much to do today."

Hair pinned, she headed to the dining room and settled to eat the food she'd requested and to drink a cup of coffee before heading to the main courtyard. Anderton was walking toward her, a small smile on his lips. "Good morning, Mrs Bonita."

She nodded and glanced around, pleased to see no one within hearing distance. "We aren't making this widely known at the moment." But a glow had settled in her chest. "We need to go to the mercantile. See if there's any substantial damage, and meet with a builder."

As she spoke, James entered the area. "Good morning, Constance. Anderton. What are your plans today?"

"I need to inspect the building and meet with a builder. We should be there for most of the day," she answered.

"I'd like to have a look later today, if I could," James said, and she cocked her head, surprised by his request. But he was Matteo's friend, so there was no reason to refuse him. Besides, he might know of other tradesmen or ways to source what she required to open the doors.

"Perhaps this afternoon? The builders should be there no later than two," she answered, and James agreed then left them.

Anderton frowned. "You intend to spend the entire day there? I have some tasks Damien and Matteo have asked me to undertake."

"I can meet with the builder by myself. Father left some instructions, so it's not a huge task." She shrugged. "There's a bit to organise, and I need to take measurements to know the lengths of tables, how many chairs and bodies I can fit. I need to consider facilities and so on. It's not like the workshop at home, so I need to know what will work best, not take a guess as I normally would. This building needs to be welcoming for the women I employ and meet their needs, so I need to put some thought around the layout of the building."

"You're already making a difference. I've heard several women talking about your plans, and there's excitement building," Anderton said as he sank his hands into his pants pocket. "But when would you like to head—"

"I think now, if you've eaten?" she said. When Anderton nodded, she smiled. "Then let's go. Father has already signed the paperwork to purchase, then he'll arrange the transfer into my name once other announcements are made." Her hand rose and she rubbed the chain around her neck. Anderton's smile grew as he nodded.

Matteo clutched the balcony as the Phoenix began its descent. He'd rather be home with his wife. *Wife.* He never would have expected such a reality to be his, neither would he have expected such a talented, smart, or beautiful woman to fill the role.

Now, however, it was his reality.

And here he was; less then twenty-four hours later, he'd left her to travel here. To the land near Casa Bonita. The place he'd grown up but would never call home.

"That's the island over there?" Damien pointed to a rocky island distant from where they would land.

"Yes. Accessible only by water. The cliffs make any kind of attack difficult. My grandfather chose well when looking for a defensible location to build his house." Matteo stared. "There's a small set of steps on the ocean-side and another on the land-side. They're steep, cut into the rock, so while you can land on the northern tip, there's little to no land. That's usually where the fisherman has his house, and there's a pulley system to deliver goods in that location, but apart from that, the house must be fully self-sufficient. There's basement storage in all the main buildings. The rule set down by my grandfather was always allow for a minimum of ninety days food on hand. That way they can weather storms, attacks, and major illness and plague. He was the quintessential planner, you might say."

"Interesting," Damien murmured. "And Lores' studio?"

Matteo pointed out a high tower. "He's located in that building. When I was here, he had the top three floors for his exclusive use. Good natural light, and out of any main traffic way."

They glanced at the buildings which all but filled the top of the craggy island. The houses were built of stone, and Matteo knew that this was how they utilised the rocks they'd quarried to build the basements.

"Well, let's see what the latest is, and see if we can find the location of your brother's vessel," Damien said, watching as the ground rose toward them. Once the Phoenix had landed, they headed for the harbour master's office.

The older man hurried out to meet them. "Mr Matteo, it's been far too many years!" Carrick, the harbour master, took hold of Matteo's hand and pumped it up and down.

"This is Mr Whitmore, and he's—"

"I've heard of him, Mr Matteo. He's the inventor of the panthera, and I've read about his unmanned boats. What an amazing invention!" Carrick extended his hand to Damien and shook it. "It's an absolute pleasure, sir. I never expected... I know your ship was here before. The Phoenix is a beauty, though when James was here, I didn't realise he was still working with Mr Matteo."

Damien smiled. "I'm sure there will be lots of opportunities to discuss my inventions, however, you're surprised about James?"

"Oh, well, when he met with Lores and that monster of his that was a woman once..." Carrick shook his head. "I know she was your sister, Mr Matteo, but she's not human, not anymore."

Matteo frowned. "Met with Lores? Are you sure?"

"Oh yes," Carrick answered. "After Mr Javier left, Lores and your friend James came here looking for Nadia and her husband, but they'd already left. And she's a nasty piece of work too," he growled. "I'd say she has plans, not that she'd tell the likes of me."

The hair on his neck stood up. James' meeting with Lores. Why? What?

Damien glanced at him, brows narrowed together. "Matteo?"

"Why would James have met with Lores?" he queried.

Carrick grimaced. "I don't know why, but I heard a whisper that they'd been in contact."

Anderton followed Constance to the door. "You're sure you're going to be fine? You'll lock the door and only allow the builders in?" He'd already shoved the actinic pistol into her hand.

"Yes, I'll stay safe, Anderton. You go. I have enough to keep me busy here."

She knew he wasn't comfortable, but they both had tasks to complete. "Go, Anderton. I promise I'll be safe."

He left and she fastened the door behind him then headed into the centre of what would become the sales area. While there was already some counter space, it wouldn't be sufficient for her needs. So, she started to draft out how she saw the space on the pad where she'd written the tasks she'd hoped to achieve for the day, along with the names of the people she'd been informed she'd be meeting. Anderton had been most insistent that she knew and checked the people she'd be talking to.

"The builder is Matthew Freeton. He's highly skilled, and he may or may not be accompanied by Joseph Mattson, his assistant. They are residents of Matteo's community, and he trusts them. They may also bring with them a plumber who will consider the placement of water connections and the bathrooms you've requested."

She scribbled the names on the pad and sighed. "All right, I have their names, Who else?"

"Matteo also arranged for the carter to come in—Bill Marr. He's been running goods between here and New York, and I guess he'll be depositing orders for you at the postal depot. He's going to need you to talk to him about collection points and how you plan to store items for him to collect, given he's likely to be travelling through early in the morning."

She rubbed her forehead. "Should I add James to the list as well?" She spoke a little acerbically then sighed. "I'm sorry, Anderton. I shouldn't snap at you."

He nodded. "It's a lot to take in, but given the situation you have to be careful."

"Okay, okay," Constance agreed. "I know you're right, but I just..." She shrugged. "I'll be careful, I promise."

. . .

She was just about to start measuring when a knock came at the door. Peering out the front window, she noted James there. "I'm coming," she called and unlocked the door.

He pushed in. "Nice. However, I need you to come with me." James grabbed her arm.

"Ow!" she said as she pushed at him. "What are you...?"

Several other men–brutal-looking, tough men—pushed into the building. "This the woman you want?" growled one of them.

"Yes. She'll be useful to us," James said, and for the first time, she noted a sneer on his face and a cold light in his eyes. "I'm very sorry to do this, Constance, but you're the chess piece I need against your father."

Her mouth dropped open. "Chess piece?"

A man hurried forward and flung a sack over her head while cruel hands picked her up.

Matteo lurched into the parlour on the Phoenix and grabbed the communicase. He dialled the compound, his nerves jumping and quivering.

"Anderton," came the voice, and Matteo exhaled.

"I need to talk to Constance."

"She's not here, Matteo. I left her at the mercantile." His guts twisted at Anderton's reply.

"Who's guarding her?" Matteo demanded.

"I left her there on her own. She locked the door behind me, and I made sure she had an actinic pistol. Why?"

He closed his eyes and said a quick, silent prayer. "Where's James?"

Anderton cleared his throat. "He headed over to the mercantile about an hour ago. She was also going to meet with the builder and plumber. Is there a problem?"

"He's been in contact with Lores," Matteo said. "Get over to her. Secure her and stay with her until we can get back." His guts twisted as Damien barrelled into the room.

"You left before—" Damien blustered.

Matteo shook his head. "She went to the mercantile and Anderton left her there. James headed over to her some time ago. I'm sending Anderton to get her."

Damien's face paled. "What?"

"Tell Damien I'm on my way," Anderton said. "I'll contact you from the automotive when I've got her."

Matteo relayed the message as he disconnected the call.

Damien swore.

"Damien, I'll kill Lores if anything happens to her." Matteo turned to his now father-in-law. "I'll hunt him down."

"Lores left yesterday, taking your sister Maria with him. Carrick said she's destructive and uncontrolled. They were travelling in a secured carriage toward Bald Head." Damien's voice shook.

Matteo shook his head, hoping it would clear the fog of terror descending. "We need to—"

"Prepare for take-off," was bellowed down the hall, and the Phoenix lurched.

Chapter Twenty-Four

CONSTANCE FOUGHT the bonds James had twined around her, and the disorientation, not to mention that the cloying sensation caused by the sack over her head increased the panic spiking.

She kicked and fought. "Let me out!" she screeched, but without success. Wherever she was, it certainly wasn't in the mercantile, as the swaying movement told her they were travelling somewhere.

Her arms and legs ached from a mixture of the unfamiliar position and how long she'd fought against her bindings.

She took a breath. *You need to focus, Constance. Information is what you need. Once you know who is in on the plan, where you're going and how, you can plan something.*

Constance stilled. Listened. What was the sound? Horses moving swiftly, or was it something more? She strained and the sound became clearer. Horses, yes. So, they were planning to move her that way.

Horse travel was slow, so there was time for Matteo to find her, catch up. How long had she been a captive? It felt like hours, but she knew terror seemed to increase the perception of time.

Suddenly the bag was removed. Sunlight, weak and dying, shone in her eyes, and she blinked, blinded by the experience. She sat in the open, on the back of a long dray, it was flanked by riders, she noted, scanning from side to side. They didn't pay her any attention, and she was thankful for the moment.

"I'm sorry, Constance. But you must understand, this was the only way to get you out of town without anyone being the wiser. Now, let me adjust your bindings. You can even sit up since no one will know where you are or hear you." James smiled, and for the first time, she was aware of a singsong thread in his voice as he crouched before her, swaying in time with the movement of the vehicle. "No one knows until I'm ready to tell, and no one will care, except maybe your father. He'll pay dearly, and I'll take control, just as I always planned to."

At least he doesn't suspect the truth of what's between Matteo and myself.

"You won't. My father isn't a fool, he'll see through your plot." She leaned forward and grinned in what she hoped was a suitably scary manner. "He'll find you, then you'll pay. It will be slow and long and painful."

"Oh dear." James smiled. "He has to overcome my secret weapon, or maybe not so secret." He leaned closer, so his breath slid over her face. "I've done a deal, a long time ago. So many things can be forgiven on the path to true power, and your father doesn't have that. The automatons your sister creates? They're lesser. A pale substitute compared to what I have."

Constance's stomach contents suddenly curdled because she knew.

"You did a deal with Lores?"

James nodded. "Of course I did. He gives me power, and I give him the freedom to continue his work. How perfect is that? Your father's pathetic pantheras are nothing compared to the power of Maria. A living, breathing automaton. See? Stronger, angrier, and almost able to think for herself." His grin was mad if the manic smile was anything to go by. "And all mine."

She gulped, because the image he conjured was terrifying in her mind. "If they think, they don't need you," she whispered.

"*Almost*, I said. I have fail-safes embedded, which I control. But for now, sit back and enjoy the view. This will take a day or two."

He turned away and clambered into the long seat at the front of the dray beside the drive, leaving her in the back, tied to a wooden board which thrust upward.

They flew fast and low, but Matteo paced back and forth, waiting for news. Any kind of news right now would give them something to work with.

Hours had passed, the moon rising over the landscape, and he considered how and where and why in his mind. How had he missed the fact that James was staying with him to gather information, supplies, and who knew what else?

Damien called, "Matteo? Anderton again. He has some news."

Matteo spun on his heel and hurried to the communicase in the parlour, scrubbing his face. "Anderton?"

"He's travelling in an open vehicle, a dray. They were seen by several leaving town, on a vehicle hauling grain. Packed high. There were riders too, maybe six or ten. The witnesses aren't totally sure how many, but they were all in agreement that they were headed in the direction of Casa Bonita."

"When did they leave, Anderton?"

Silence dragged out. "It was quick after I left. Probably no more than a half an hour."

"Right." Matteo looked into the distance, not really seeing the room, but considering what he knew. Horses like that moved slowly, but if they off-loaded the grain, they could move faster. He looked at his father-in-law and asked, "Can the automotive travel off-road?"

Damien shook his head. "Not at any speed. We built it for travelling on formed roads and tracks. This is likely overland, and horses would be faster."

Matteo swore. "Is there anything else I should know?"

Anderton said, "We found a communicase in the bunkhouse, along with a notation book. He'd been in close contact with Lores for over a year. I... Hang on a moment."

Matteo could hear murmurs, and he waited impatiently for more information.

"We have news," Anderton announced. "The grain was dumped out of town, about five miles out at a staging point, and there was a single dray with six outriders. They're moving slowly though, because one of the horses was lamed leaving town. They've four horses as there were no fresh replacements, so they left two behind."

Considering this, Matteo growled. "So, we can estimate it would take them four to five days to reach Casa Bonita. Lores and Maria have a head start of a day or two. It's likely they'll meet sometime tomorrow." The knowledge burned him.

"We need to find them before Lores does," Damien agreed.

"It's worse than that. It seems he's promised Constance to Lores. To do with as he pleases. It's all here in his notes. He doesn't know..." Anderton's words trailed off, and Matteo heard flipping pages through the receiver of the communicase. "Hang on, he's going to give her to him unless Damien hands over the specs to his inventions, including the engines and the controls for the pantheras."

"He doesn't know she's mine," growled Matteo. "I'll find him and crush him." Fury and terror pulsed through him in equal parts.

"We will crush him," Damien added. "Captain! Man the searchlights! We'll set up a grid. Anderton, board my other ship and bring men. We'll sort this once and for all," he bit out. "Then we'll finish the houses. Without Lores, they don't have access to the munitions. I'm also bringing in Francesca and Raphael."

Dawn edged ever closer as Constance woke from her light doze. You can't do more than that when you're trussed to a stake like a turkey, she thought sourly. The need of her body to rid itself of the contents of her bladder was also rearing its head. Ignore it.

Silence reigned, and she carefully moved closer to the stake, moving left and right in silent efforts to free herself. The ropes held, but the stake was weak. If she could just manage to get it free, she might have a chance, especially as they hadn't rebound her feet after the last 'comfort stop' as James had termed it.

It was laborious, and more than once she ceased her movements as a man snored or grunted.

Moments passed as she squirmed and tugged, and finally it slid free.

Sweat soaked her body, but there wasn't time to worry about that. Thank God Damien had insisted they learn survival and fighting skills. The lessons he'd thrust upon them—especially after Francesca's abduction—were now coming into their own.

It took more squirming to tug herself free of the stake, and as moments ticked by, she was aware time was bleeding away. She still needed to find shelter, somewhere they wouldn't look.

She scanned the horizon and noted that the dirt track was open, with straggly stands of shrubby trees here and there. Where could she hide?

Biting her lip, she slid from the dray and headed off toward the stands of trees; perhaps they hid some kind of arroyo or sandy area where she could hide? Her body screamed with pain, and the way her arms remained pinned behind her kept her off-balance.

Reaching the tree line, she wanted to sob. There was nothing that would hide her from view, and she didn't have time to look for a way to release the ropes at her back, so she shuffled on, scanning the horizon.

Tears dripped down her face as she hunted franticly, looking for anything that would hide her from view. Her chest ached and her legs shook as she moved, one step after another. Any moment and the men would wake, find her missing.

A sound echoed, breaking through the silence, and she gazed up, seeing an amazing sight. A dirigible... fast, gleaming copper in the sunlight.

A loud shout came as the men woke and realised she'd escaped.

"Help!" Constance lurched out from the questionable cover of the trees. "Help me!" she screamed.

Pandemonium broke out from the men, then she heard a bang!

Whatever it was thudded into her, the force driving her to the ground. "Help me!" The last scream died away as pain radiated and the blackness dragged her under.

Watching through the occular, Matteo saw the movements, saw the moment she fell, the red staining her shirt. "Constance! Set us down. Get us down now! They've shot her!"

It felt like his heart was straining against his skin, and Matteo dropped the lens.

The dirigible dropped rapidly, and he had to hold onto the balcony as they plummeted in a controlled manner toward the ground. Even before the men deployed the emergency ramp, he was gripping a rope and rappelling down toward her. "Let the pantheras out!" His bellow had the men racing, and he knew Damien wasn't far behind him.

He pelted toward where she lay, crumpled on the ground. His hand found the pulse of her neck. "She's still alive," he called as another man, the one the captain had informed him had medical training, pushed him aside.

"Let me see." The man's hand shook. "It's bad. We need to get her back to the Phoenix, but we need a pallet of some kind. We need to move her carefully." Even as he spoke, he shoved wads of material hard against the wound and began binding it. "I'm not sure how long this will work," he muttered, and Matteo glared at the man.

"You're supposed to be trained—"

"In the things that usually go wrong on a dirigible. Not gunshot wounds. Go back to the ship, organise a pallet." The man spoke rapidly. "We don't have time for anything else."

Screams echoed, and Matteo ignored them. The outcome of the men who'd abducted her was far less important than ensuring her survival. He ran, as fast as his legs could pump, back to the ship. He gave the commands and waited as the necessary items were assembled. The captain had the men decrease the angle of the ramp by making it longer, and he recognised on one level that was to make loading her simpler for everyone.

The men raced back to her, and while he wanted to follow, his body betrayed him. Weakness filled his muscles, leaving them soft like an over-ripe lettuce leaf. His chest bellowed as he watched the careful way the men loaded Constance onto the pallet.

"She's tough, Matteo." Damien patted him on the back, but the ineffectual pats merely reinforced how he'd let her down.

"Damien, I can't lose her." Inside his chest, the pain was a rictus, growing and spiralling. He shoved his balled fists deep into his pockets as the men carrying her ran to the ship as the second ship arrived. Matteo wanted to follow them to the medical room, but Damien held him back.

"I'm going to go give directions. Wait for me. Don't leave me behind," he muttered, and Matteo nodded.

Chapter Twenty-Five

SHE BURNED; Constance twisted as the fire extended throughout her body. The light scorched her eyes, and she tried to pull away from it.

Something wet and cooling was in her mouth, and she eagerly sucked. A hand slid over her forehead and a cooling pad was placed there. She wanted more, tried to ask, but darkness surrounded her again.

Matteo clutched Constance's hand. "She's not getting any better."

Francesca bustled around the room. "There's nothing more we can do right now. Keep bathing her, and give her the sponge to suck on when she's conscious. All we can do is wait for the fever to break." She lifted the cover over the wound site. "There's no redness. It's just the body's way of coping." She shrugged. "But you need a break."

He shook his head. "I'm staying. She needs me."

Francesca—the older, darker-haired, half-sister of Constance—squatted down beside him. "No. She needs someone to care for her, but you need rest. You're no good if you're unwell or exhausted. I'll stay with her. She won't be alone, and if the fever breaks while you rest, we'll come for you. I promise."

He rubbed shaking hands over gritty, sore eyes. "But I can't abandon—"

"You're not abandoning her. Go rest. She'll be here waiting for you when you wake." She cocked her head to one side. "She's not going to die, it's not that severe, I'm sure."

He exhaled and rose unsteadily, pushed past Francesca who settled into the seat he'd just vacated. "An hour."

"Two. And a bath. Perhaps even a meal and a shave. We'll call if she wakes or something changes."

He nodded and left the room. Damien accosted him outside. "How is she?"

"Delirious still, but I've been sent to bed," Matteo answered.

"It's been nearly two days," Damien growled. "Surely by now..."

"Francesca said she won't die."

Damien's eyes closed, as if he were saying a prayer of thankfulness. Matteo understood that sentiment.

"James? Lores? Maria?" Matteo asked.

He'd been locked in the medical room since Constance had been shot, and he'd left Damien to cope with the fallout. Anything else was of little concern. His world was in there, and he glanced in the direction of the medical room.

"Maria was shot during the skirmish. She died, Matteo. I'm... I'm sorry."

Matteo shook his head, allowing himself to accept the truth he'd ignored for years. "She's been gone really for years. The creature that Lores created wasn't my sister anymore. Still, I can feel sorry that she's deceased. I'll arrange a decent burial for her."

Damien nodded. "Lores is wounded and enroute to Bloom on my other craft. Whether he'll survive..." Damien shook his head. "He tried to capture a panthera. Likely he wanted to dissect the machine, but it didn't end well for him. If he survives, and it's not certain, he'll never be the same again. James is in custody."

"Then Casa Bonita is under Javier's rule still."

"We have news. Javier is going to recover, but he's surrendered the house, financial assets, and so on to Bloom. He's taking control of all the armaments, and I'm sending my sons to assist. The assets are to be distributed among the residents and yourself. You will also receive control of the property itself."

"I don't want it." He genuinely didn't.

"You could sell it." Damien smiled. "I know someone looking for an asset just like that."

Matteo frowned. "Who?"

"We need a secure location for housing their prisoners."

He considered the man opposite him. "Prisoners?"

"There's more than a few as we dismantle the houses, and we need a secure location to keep them. Besides, now that Bloom is retiring..." Damien sighed. "I don't know why I agreed to take over."

Raphael entered the parlour and snorted. "You accepted it because, like the rest of us, Haven House is where those most important part of our lives began. And with the assistance of the fund, there's money to make a difference to those who need to rebuild their lives, not just wage war." Raphael levered himself into the seat opposite. "Francesca?"

"She's in with Constance. Matteo's going to rest, then when things have improved, we need to sit down. There are plans to make, a council to build, and a future to sculpt." Damien steepled his hands.

Matteo lurched out of the room. He would allow himself an hour. Cleanse his body and return to Constance's side. He couldn't sleep, not until he'd seen her awake.

Constance opened her eyes slowly. Cool air blew over her body. When she tried to ask for water, the words refused to emerge. Instead, she croaked.

"Constance?" Matteo's voice echoed in the cool dimness. A cloth was thrust at her, but she pushed it away.

"Dr.... Dr... ink." She couldn't ignore the sensation of being parched, and when he passed an invalid cup to her, she sipped. Grateful as the cool liquid slid down her throat.

"Slowly," he growled and pulled the cup away. "More in a minute, I promise."

His hand slid with a gentleness over her forehead, pushing away strands of hair sticking to her forehead.

"I must... look like... a fright." The weakness in her voice was most unwelcome. "What... happened?"

"James and his men shot you. You took a fever. It's been four days, Constance," he said, his voice cracking. "I was so afraid I'd lose you." He cupped her cheek. "But you're on the road to recovery now. Francesca said..." He sighed.

"Francesca's here?" She licked her dry lips and nearly sighed when he slid the cup against her mouth again.

"Yes. Caring for you. Raphael and your father have captured the men, including Lores."

"Your brother?" Wasn't it Javier who was in charge? It was all pretty wobbly in her mind.

"He capitulated. He's turned over all the assets to Bloom."

She considered the answer, then her mind settled on something else. "So, you're free now?"

Matteo smiled. "Sort of. Casa Bonita was given to me. I'm selling it. We'll never be rich, but..."

Constance smiled then reached up and cupped the hand on her cheek. "I don't want to be rich like that. I'm already rich. I have you."

He leaned down and kissed her. It was soft and sweet and full of promise.

Epilogue

CONSTANCE GRIPPED Matteo's hand as they watched the ceremony. Bloom handing over control of Bloom's council to Damien. In the last three months, much had changed. With the capture of Lores, who'd now entered the prison island of Prigione, renamed from Casa Bonita, as a long-term inmate. Javier had been granted a place at a lower security prison and was serving his life sentence as well.

As for James? He'd escaped and run, but he hadn't got far. The pantheras had cornered him and he'd died rather than face recapture.

She glanced around the room. Others who'd fought against the houses were gathered in the ballroom. The vaulted ceilings of the Whitmore Mansion were the perfect backdrop for an event such as this. Chairs and tables filled the room, with long, white tablecloths, the scent of floral displays, and the chink of crystal wine glasses.

Muted chatter filled the room as they waited for the dignitaries to complete the signing of the charter that laid out the responsibilities of council and its elected officials.

Her happiness was balanced with the weight of Matteo's grief. The one person he'd thought had been his friend had ultimately sought only to further his own ends. James had damaged a central part of his trust.

There was a new facet to the hardness Matteo carried like a shield. Only those closest to him now saw the real, caring man beneath.

It wasn't that he made people think he didn't care, but the wariness now was the first layer enveloping his heart.

"That mind of yours is working too hard again," Matteo whispered.

Her laugh was clear and full of mirth, and she shook her head, dispelling the thoughts which saddened her. "I can't help it, there's something momentous about today. Seeing the work that's been done by Francesca with the board of medical registration taking a stand against unnecessary enhancements. Damien taking control of the council, and both you and Raphael's election. These are events that will change our world."

He huffed. "Amaryllis is looking very pleased with herself too," Matteo pointed out.

She glanced at Damien's wife and her adoptive mother, still young yet a matron of their emerging society. "She's ecstatic now that she's got the funding for the orphanages and women's refuges agreed. They all..." She shook her head. "You all have achieved great things." She smiled at him. "The opportunities that will open to the women and children is gratifying as is the knowledge that no longer will houses command such power to make decisions for everyone within them. It's good to see the government officials are here to give weight to today's actions."

Matteo looked out over the table, raised a hand to one, then another of the men seated further down. More than one government official strolled by and congratulated him before moving on, along the table. "You're not without your own milestones. Now that the mercantile is open, it's amazing what you've achieved in a couple of months."

"It's small scale, Matteo." And it was. She'd hired fifteen women so far, with twelve currently being upskilled sufficiently that they could take on roles within the sewing and fitting rooms. Another four had been taken on to work on the ballistafabric suits, fulfilling a government order. The first, she hoped, of many.

He shook his head. "No. You're giving them a chance at a trade, a future. A life for their children. It's what you do. You see the need, you create amazing things, and don't think I haven't noticed the new gowns in your wardrobe."

She blushed a little. "They're a little bigger than normal though."

He smirked. "I noticed. Was there something you planned to tell me?"

From her pocket she withdrew a piece of paper. "Maybe you need to read this. Francesca wrote it for you."

He read the missive and smiled. "Five months, hmm? That should about give us time to complete the upstairs apartment."

"It won't fit us for long though, will it?"

Matteo dragged her close. "No, but that's something we can talk about once the time is right. For now, you and I and the little one will be content."

Constance smiled. She was more than content. Her life was full, she had a gift she'd never expected, and more to come. The houses that had shadowed their world for so long were no more. The shadows in her mind were replaced by the rays of light that hope brought.

The End.

Genevieve is many things, but no single title fits her quite as accurately as *'mutt'*—the one bestowed by her vicious ex-boyfriend. She's built a life, far from the family who've disowned her—one she's proud of—as a police officer with the Paranormal Liaison Division, and hiding from the world.

David is brittle from his experiences with his ex-wife Alexa, the truth his parents duped him his whole life, and he's trying to come to terms with the fallout of those beliefs, running a nest and feeling like an imposter.

A chance meeting between Genevieve and David opens up an opportunity for hope amid the grim realities of paranormal warfare.

Trusting each other may be their only choice, but the past always bites back and this time is no different.

———————————————

"Do you know anything about...?" David waved his arm, and Daniel shook his head.

David clamped his arm on his shoulder and squeezed. He knew he was pale, but the reality of the situation impinged.

Hope had glanced at him, smiled tremulously, but didn't approach.

"Are you okay?" Daniel's question swam through David's brain.

He cleared his throat, considered the man before him. "I don't... I'm resigning my commission and plan to seek a place in a new house." The words erupted from him, but once out, David relaxed.

Daniel frowned. "Today?"

He shook his head. "No. When the mess with Attar is done. I've hung in only because... It was Hope who kept me together once I came to terms with what had been done. I treated her badly and so did my parents, and I feel dirty because I believed everything I was told. Now it's hard to stay after..." David shrugged.

"But if Hope forgives you, surely the situation can be resolved?"

"No, Daniel. Everyone knows what I did. What *we* did. How we took her—Alexa's—side and left Hope to suffer the consequences of the lies. It just... it doesn't feel right, you know? She's built something good and true. I can't muddy it any longer than necessary. She needs to rebuild her life free of that taint."

Daniel frowned. "If you need to move, you would be more than welcome with me. I can talk to Javed..."

"No. But thank you." David shook his head. "When it's done... Once Attar is defeated, I'm thinking of going somewhere else."

Sucking in a deep breath, he stepped back around Daniel and wandered to the other side of the room.

Several Months Later

David looked down at his hands. Instead of the neatly manicured nails he'd always sported, ragged edges betrayed the rage he'd held at bay over the last several months.

Now this. The parchment paper in his grip crackled, and he released the hold slightly, forcing himself to read the front page.

Referring to the decree made in this cause... the marriage between the aforementioned Plaintiff and Defendant be dissolved unless sufficient cause be shown to the court...

He wasn't unhappy with the outcome. Neither was he ecstatic. It wasn't the way he'd planned for his life to proceed.

Alexa had lied to him. Made a dupe of him. There'd been no child, and she'd blinded him to truths he should have noted. The betrayal ran deep. She'd colluded with his father, alienated his mother, and damaged the relationship he had with his sister.

The situation felt untenable, really.

But still... The life he'd planned to make was over. Deleted with the stroke of a pen by a Family Court judge.

Slumping back into his chair, David surveyed the room. It was new, pale-coloured walls in a strange boxlike building, yet there was a charm to it. The kind he hadn't ever felt in the old-world manor where he'd grown to adulthood.

He sighed.

Dawn had passed some three hours before, and while he, along with his master, Javed, had agreed the house didn't require an external office set-up at this point, it felt odd to be ordering a coffee and still wearing the lounging pants he'd tugged on after showering at nine in the morning.

The phone buzzed and broke the internal ruminations that occupied his mind.

He answered with a curt "David."

"Sir, we have an officer of the law here. They say it's important they speak with you. Something to do with a situation with the vampires."

"Fine. Give me a moment, then send him in."

"Her, sir."

He blinked. "Of course."

Letting go of the button, he rose from his chair, straightened his clothing—the teachings of his mother still held tight—before lowering himself into the chair, preparing for whatever came to pass.

The door opened, and a slim, dark-haired woman entered the room. She wasn't tall, and her features were regular. Her hair, tied into a neat and tidy braid, was dark brown, though her eyes were a golden green colour.

The impressive creases, carefully aligned in her uniform, and the shine of her shoes told him she was either a new officer or one of those committed to her job. He had a feeling it was the second option.

"David Jardin?"

He inclined his head, and the woman stood, facing him.

Discomfort flowed. In his world, you asked women to sit; they were coddled and kept at home until they married. This woman might look soft, but he noted a spark of something in her eyes and the ramrod straightness of her spine. This was no meek and biddable woman here. It was perverse, but he didn't offer the seat.

"You wanted to talk to me about the vampire attacks?"

She blinked. "Uh, yes. I wanted to make some further enquiries. My name's Officer Fernly, from the Liaison Division, and I need to check some facts to determine—"

His brow furrowed as he concentrated on what had taken place the evening before. He'd found a briefing paper on his desk when he'd entered that morning.

"Oh yes," he interrupted. Something about this woman put him on guard.

She flipped open the tiny notepad she carried. "We have reports of a man attacked by what he believes was a vampire. He escaped, but it terrified him. He's lost a lot of blood and may very well require assistance coming to terms with the attack."

"And what do you want me to do for you today, Officer Fernly?"

"It's been suggested that it's more than just a single attack. We haven't been informed of such a circumstance, and if there's a likelihood of danger to the public—"

He raised a hand. "I'm limited on what I can divulge, Officer." Now he indicated to a seat and watched as she slowly lowered herself to the padded cushion. The closing of her eyes and the gentle exhalation betrayed her emotional state.

"You were on duty last night and attended this call. Yet you're on duty this morning."

The woman seated opposite him glanced in his direction. "I work the hours necessary to get the job done."

Available from Love Books Publishing
books2read.com/ImmortalConsequences

Direct Autographed Copy
https://www.imogenenix.net/AsDawnBreaks

Tia's Redemption

When you need a job done, you need a woman.

Tia—codename Cat—knows all about loss. Orphaned at a young age, she's made it through a series of foster homes, with one single aim in sight. Joining the Australian army. Now an accomplished sniper with the *Alathea Rangers*—an all-woman team, begun in Greece and now based in America—covert operations team, she's found where she belongs. Or has she?

When she's sent to retrieve the child of an Australian diplomat, she drops into Zabuti—an unstable African country — with no illusions about her importance in the greater scheme of things.

When Cal sees Cat's landing, he's unsure about the man. His misgivings are even more grave when he realises Cat's female. Can this slight woman do the job? He's supposed to be her in-country guide, but though he packs a gun and is a CIA operative, he can't keep them safe.

The stakes are raised on the wild race across Zabuti, and nothing can prepare him for what's to come, including the passion that rises between them.

In the end, nothing is certain, including their survival.

Tia dragged herself from the pool, chest heaving and arms shaking. "Fifty fucking laps. I did it." Once on the concrete, she slumped, ignoring the scratch and the wet patch.

"Mum'll have a cow because you're swearing again," called Vanessa, her much younger foster sister.

Tia closed her eyes. *One-one hundred, two-one hundred.* It wasn't that Vanessa was difficult. She was just young and still very innocent.

Tia knew the house rules, so there wasn't any way she could claim ignorance after seventeen and a half months.

Hell, she'd been through a myriad of similar arguments already—at least four other times. But this was her last foster care placement. Only three weeks left of school to go; then she'd be gone and on her own. *Freedom never felt sweeter*, she silently acknowledged. The letter she'd been waiting for arrived yesterday, confirming she'd made it through the rigorous army intake process.

"Sorry," she muttered, knowing full well if she didn't, Vanessa would tell, and all Tia wanted now was an easy transition out of care. She pushed up from the ground. "We should go home."

Vanessa's eyes drew together. "What about your run?"

Tia couldn't restrain the laugh. "I did that while you were still asleep, kiddo. This morning. Five kilometres isn't a lot in the grand scheme of things, you know." And it wasn't when you only slept five to six hours a night. Less when memories haunted her.

Even now, after years of therapy, they still cropped up, stressed her like sitting final exams or waiting for a letter that would ultimately allow her to start her life.

Tia stepped over to her bag where it sat on the polished aluminium seating and slid into the coverall she'd stashed at the top. Then she tugged the rope handles of the canvas bag over her shoulder.

Tia stared at the younger girl, hoping she'd wordlessly gather her swim bag. At eleven, Vanessa was cute but pushy, with curling blonde hair and sweet blue eyes to fit the round face and Cupid's bow lips. *When she grows up, the boys will be lining up.*

The only natural child of her foster carer, Vanessa had seen kids come and go and handled it like a pro. Not that Tia was concerned. She treated her the same way she treated her classmates. Did what she had to but nothing more. Encouraging any kind of lasting relationship wasn't on Tia's radar.

"Mummy said you got a letter from the army. When are you leaving?"

It took Tia every ounce of willpower not to retort "as soon as possible" and instead answered, "Three weeks, kiddo."

"But you'll come back and see us, right? Like some of the others?" Vanessa didn't whine so much as attack the words as a fact. That set Tia's teeth on edge.

"Maybe," she muttered as she unlocked the aging Toyota she'd bought with money given by the executors of her parents' will. There was more, but she kept it stashed for the proverbial "rainy day" she was sure would come at some point. "Come on. Get in and buckle up. You've got homework, and I need to get my dress out for tonight."

The leaver's dinner was one small highlight in the lead-up to getting out of this central Queensland town that she wouldn't forego. It was a rite of passage. She'd even sprung for her hair to be styled this afternoon and her make-up to be applied.

Available from Love Books Publishing
books2read.com/Tias-Redemption

Direct Autographed Copy
https://imogenenix.net/product/tias-redemption/

Warriors of the Elector
Book One

The first time Elara laid eyes on Grayson was when he rescued her from the clutches of a madman and his scientists who were kidnapping humans and conducting horrific experiments on them. That was years ago. In spite of her attempts to deepen their relationship, they remained nothing more than close friends. Now Elara is a medic with the Admiralty, and she knows what she wants. It's been Grayson since the beginning. When Elara is stationed on the *Star of Ishtar*, she arrives with a plan to further her career. But this time her plan has an added bonus—to finally get her man.

Grayson's spent years fighting the connection between himself and Elara. He's certain it only exist because he saved her life. But his will is failing, and he fears he just might give in to temptation.

"I finally made it." Elara Sudonne watched as the hull of the *Star of*

Ishtar loomed in the inky darkness. She clutched her hands tightly together as the shuttle approached the hulking battleship.

This would be her new home and first combat ST placement for the Earth Empire. She quaked inwardly with nerves but fought to keep her serene exterior. Previously her deployments had consisted solely of on-planet expeditions and in rehabilitation and dirtside facilities. When the chance had arisen to move to the battleship, she'd grabbed it with both hands.

The frigid air chilled her bones as she sat in her shuttle seat, but a trickle of sweat inched its way down her back under the fresh gray wool flight uniform. Little puffs of vapor escaped her mouth as she rubbed her arms. Nerves stretched tight, she looked through the small portal at the front of the vessel. She wanted to tug at the collar that somehow seemed to have grown tighter as the ship loomed ahead, but instead she firmed her mouth, straightened her spine, and concentrated on the future.

"So damned long." She'd been working toward this outcome since the day Grayson Myatt and Duvall McCord had saved her from her Ru'Edan captors. She was lucky, she'd survived the 'experimentation' of the Ru'Edan leader Crick Sur Banden's scientists. "And all I have to remind me are my scars." She didn't grin at her own joke.

The person seated behind her jostled but she ignored it, lost in her memories. On that day, so very long ago, the young Elara, fresh-faced and with idealistic views of the empire, was taken from the mall where she'd been shopping with friends, thrust into the back of a transport vehicle, and given to the Ru'Edan scientists to experiment on.

For days they'd worked on her and others, seeking an average pain threshold of humans, slicing her skin then noting reactions and how long it took to heal. They'd cut her arms, body, and even her face, and now she carried the extensive scarring of the exercise as a reminder to herself and others of what they were fighting for. Freedom. The freedom of Earth and its allied planets.

She'd never relinquished hope, it had been her constant companion as she fought against the all-consuming terror. Then they'd found her in that dirty, disused warehouse. They'd found others too, in various states of death and decay. The smells of despair had filled the air with a fetid ripeness that she'd never been able to forget.

Since that day she'd promised herself that she would pay the Ru'Edan back for what they'd done to her. What they'd taken from her. Over the years, she tempered and honed the rage while remaining adamant that she would see the final act played out. She couldn't physically fight, but she had learned about trauma, knew it and understood how it affected a person, and used it as a weapon.

The iron will forged through her experiences had fed her determination, and she'd applied herself to study, finishing in the top ten percent of her class. She entered the medical program at the academy, working hard to excel. Her family remained supportive if perplexed as to why she had chosen to keep reminding herself of what had happened.

The maw of the *Star of Ishtar* loomed closer, opening its cavernous mouth as she watched through the portal. She could hear the voices of the shuttle crew signaling their intention to enter and land, the tinny confirmation coming swiftly. She watched avidly while the shuttle manoeuvered, imagining the invisible shields dropping to allow it entry.

Her hands twisted with fear and anger, but she tamped down her emotions. Anger never helped anyone. Staying strong, knowing your history, and ensuring it couldn't be repeated, they were the answers, she told herself firmly, pulling herself from the grip of a dark past so horrific she still saw it in her dreams. She pushed it away to the recesses of her mind and focused on what she was about to do.

A squark overhead, the usual mechanical sound that alerted all on board to a transmission by the captain, caught her attention. "Attention all passengers. We are entering the shuttle bay. Please ensure when you disembark you remove all personal items. Move beyond the white line and wait for your designation."

The lights of the bay flashed as they entered, and once again Elara marveled at how far humanity had moved since they had first walked the Earth. She saw the opening of the structure as the shuttle moved into the bay, inching forward slowly until it stopped its ponderous motion and began its descent to the floor. Something deep inside warmed even as the shuttle's environmental systems began to synchronise with the cooler temperature of the *Star of Ishtar*, and she felt a smile crawl its way over her face.

Elara breathed in deeply, inhaling the metallic-tasting, recycled air and welcoming the calmness that settled on her body. Her eyes closed as she filled her lungs. "I'm here." There was more than a little satisfaction in her tone, and she smiled. She slowly exhaled, finding that centre of peace she relied on.

A loud thud and clank echoed as the deep drone split the air. The engines were powering down, and there she was, on one of the Earth Empire's Emeritus class battleships. She sat in her seat, waiting for the all clear from the captain, and once it sounded through the cabin, she rose, tugging at the webbing belt and disengaging it.

The small backpack beside her was all she carried as she made her way to the exit, not needing to duck as so many others did. She stepped through the door, her hands gripping the rail of the cold, metal stairs which connected to the side of the grey shuttle.

She clambered down them slowly, savoring the experience. The sting of the cold on her hands from the stairs, frigid from even their brief exposure to the blackness of space, made her flinch inwardly. The shuttle journey from the Admiralty's strategic base at Aenna to their current position had taken just over an hour, but the whole time it felt like her heart had been in her throat. Her mouth was dry as she followed the new recruits from the ship into the landing bay. She stopped, silently noting the slight mustiness of the air, the recycled quality easily recognizable. Everything, including the oxygen, needed recycling in space.

All around her people swarmed, either around the ships or into the dogleg line that now formed ahead of her. Someone had opened the baggage locker of the shuttle, and the sound of dropping bags hitting the plascrete floor echoed in the air. Another crewmember guided trolleys to the other side of the shuttle, pulling out boxes with important day-to-day items for the ship, including vaccines and plants. She watched briefly, all the while listening to the alien cacophony. Voices called in welcome to old crewmembers, while new ones watched, many goggle-eyed in the fresh uniforms of newly minted officers and crewmembers.

Her gaze flicked around quickly, taking in the sights, sounds, and smells, pungent with oils and grease; burning smells from the scorched plascrete and the press of sweaty or nervous bodies. She joined the line silently, tacking onto the end, and stayed at parade rest, knowing the welcoming voice would cut through the air soon enough. She felt somehow disconnected from the main throng. Perhaps the knowledge that this was the outcome she had worked for years to achieve set her apart. However, still, she felt so...distant from everything around her. She smiled secretly at the bout of whimsy.

"Attention!" The voice boomed out over the plascrete of the docking bay, and she snapped her body into position, noting the commander who had bellowed the words. Technically, she outranked most members aboard the *Star of Ishtar*, except for the command and leadership staff, but she knew all newcomers had to join the welcoming parade, regardless of rank.

Fleet Captain Elphin came into view, his tired features topped by salt-and-pepper grey hair, which highlighted his cool blue eyes. Elara also recognised a body prone to a little middle-aged thickness. Following behind him was his second-in-command, Duvall McCord. A young up-and-coming officer, his status as a fast-tracking officer heading toward his own command, with Elphin both his mentor and captain, had become almost legendary at the academy.

She looked closely at McCord, noting the dynamic drive of his actions and movements. Soon he would achieve a promotion to captain, and she rejoiced for her friend. She'd followed his career with interest and had to tamp down a smile as his eyes betrayed the shock of seeing her before settling into their flat command persona. So he hadn't been apprised of her deployment, she noted, and she had to restrain the tiny feeling of surprise and satisfaction. She filed that snippet of information away.

She caught sight of the man standing behind Duvall. Grayson Myatt. He'd made her heart beat faster for years. Tall and blond with a muscular build and a sexy, tight, little butt, he had pools of deep-blue eyes that had always made her think of forever. He had a growth of stubble on his chiseled jaw, and her fingers itched to touch his perfect lips. Yes, since the day he'd found her in that nasty warehouse tied down like a ragged animal, she'd worshipped him from afar.

Now she had her opportunity to tangle with him, hopefully much closer than any chance that had ever come her way before. With a sigh, she pulled her gaze back to the captain and forced herself to concentrate on his words. She couldn't afford to have her commanding officer angry due to her being distracted.

"Welcome to the *Star of Ishtar*. Most academy recruits want to join us because of what we represent, but on this ship, we only take the best of the best. So, if you made it here, you're the ones we wanted to take a look at. Getting here is only the first step. Staying here is harder to achieve. Our people are the best. Earn your place, and in return, we'll make you one of our crew—a member of the *Star of Ishtar*. Only the best and the brightest wear our uniform and badge. You'll be expected to perform to your absolute limit then give some more. We don't tolerate people who don't pull their weight. Do us proud and wear your uniform with pride." The captain looked out over the new members of his crew. His voice had echoed during his speech, and now it died away.

He scanned the faces before him, and she could almost read his thoughts. There were new security officers and a smattering of other crew. Some of them were young and impressionable, and she knew a few wouldn't make the cut as crewmembers. Others would carve out their place on the *Star of Ishtar* and move to better positions and placements, like she would: the new SurgiTech, a younger female, experienced but untried on board a ship. She smiled at that thought.

Some of those who stood with her would be replaced as they failed the exacting standards the captain set. She'd heard that he was a firm captain, fair but demanding. He'd have to be to command this ship. The Ishtar had well over five hundred at full capacity, and the captain could select their placements as his command staff saw fit from the many who applied to join the crew. She sensed his satisfaction with the choices in the relaxation of his body.

Abruptly, he turned to Duvall, breaking her study of him. "Get them to where they need to present themselves." His words echoed as he walked away. He had a purposeful stride. Quick but unhurried, like he knew where he was going and how to get there. A man who knew how to get what he wanted. Someone to respect and admire.

"My name is Commander Duvall McCord. I am your second-in-command, and my direct subordinate is Commander Grayson Myatt. While you are aboard the *Star of Ishtar* you will be required to fulfill your duties efficiently. As Captain Elphin said, do your job right and you will be one of ours, with all the benefits that come with being a crewmember of the *Star of Ishtar*."

He paused and eyeballed each of the newer recruits, those fresh from the academy. Many of them paled under his gaze, and she smiled inwardly. Even the older people in the line seemed to quake beneath his scowl. He'd always had that air of innate authority, even when barely out of the academy himself. She knew his methods and watched him make full use of the carefully practiced tone of presence.

"Each of you has been assigned. You will present yourselves to the chief of your section. Those details will be found in your orders. Commander Myatt has organised a team to escort you to your cabins. You will have approximately one hour to prepare. We've arranged for crewmembers to escort you to your superiors. Be ready to present for duty. Any issues, you will, of course, take up with your section commander. Should there be need to take any further action, you will see Commander Myatt. You should only see me if you are a command crewmember or as a point of discipline. I am not one for small talk, so if you present to me, have a very good reason."

He delivered the words slowly and deliberately, and Elara restrained a small smile on hearing at least one gulp from those in the line nearest her.

"We run a tight ship here. Discipline and commitment are the two key factors we look for beyond loyalty in our crew. You will from henceforth represent our ship everywhere, and we do not tolerate anything less than the best." He looked around once more, the stern demeanor he wore so well reinforcing the message. If she hadn't known him for so long, she too might have missed the hint of humor glinting in his eyes, the one many took for coldness.

Her legs ached, and she wanted to move and relieve the pressure on them, but she held herself still, waiting for the command to dismiss. She wouldn't let herself or him down now. Not after she'd worked so long to achieve this position.

As the new ST, she had no previous experience on ships. She had vast experience in the field, but Elara was aware that would count for little in the eyes of most of the crew. She didn't intend to signal a weakness to anyone and least of all on her first day aboard the *Star of Ishtar*. That thought held her still and controlled.

She had big shoes to fill after her predecessor, Jamieson, had retired, even though she knew she could fill the void he'd left behind. As a long-term member of the crew—over twenty years—his tenure on the *Star of Ishtar* had placed him aboard since its launch. Due to his experience in the heat of battle with the Ru'Edan he had made a name for himself as the coldest of cold in the hottest of situations. She hoped to emulate that herself and carve out her own place aboard the Ishtar, as its crew lovingly knew her.

Duvall and Grayson knew how much she wanted to prove herself. They just wouldn't have expected it here, on the Ishtar.

She watched Duvall study her, then, quickly turning on his heel, call to those assembled, "Dismissed."

Once they started to move away, she softened her stance, preparing to turn when the call came.

"Sudonne! A moment if you please."

Elara turned to face Duvall. "Commander?"

"Welcome to the *Star of Ishtar*, Elara. While I am surprised you're the new ST, Grayson and I are pleased you could join us. But how did you manage to pull it off? Keeping it quiet that you were the new ST?" he asked, his voice deep enough to make most women shiver with anticipation.

She smiled, thinking it was a shame she didn't have any feelings for him except sisterly attachment, but then again, given his lack of deep commitment to women, maybe it wasn't such a shame after all.

She understood what drove him. He wanted his own ship and to captain his own future. They'd spent many nights over wine or ale discussing his beliefs that commitment grounded a person. Inwardly, she shrugged. He'd make those calls for himself, though she was sure that one day he would come across someone who would make him consider his choices a little more thoroughly.

"I'm pleased to be here, Duvall. Having an uncle who happens to be an admiral, he was able to let Captain Elphin know that I wanted to surprise you. It's a small world in the Admiralty. Elphin already knew of me, so he okayed my placement. Once the powers knew there was no impediments to me joining the crew, it was fairly simple from there." She felt a small smile creep onto her face, then let it drop away. "What do you think Grayson thinks?"

"Ah, still chasing him, are you?" He grinned, his eyes twinkling. "I think he'll be pleased you're finally old enough and you're here." He looked her straight in the eye. "But you may just need to remind him of that particular fact." He motioned for her to go before him, barking out a deep laugh. "Come on, I'll show you to your cabin."

Available from Love Books Publishing
Available in Ebook via Books2Read

Direct Autographed Copy
https://www.imogenenix.net/Warriors1

The Blood Bride
Blood Secrets Book 1

Hope just wants to be an ordinary nestling. She went to college and escaped, but now she's back and there's a secret everyone is keeping from her.

Xavier is the new master of the nest, ready to welcome home the daughter of the house who he has never met. He's unprepared for the woman who steals his breath and enchants him.

Now Hope and Xavier must fight for lives and those of the innocents. After all, it is only by overcoming the rogues that they will have a chance of a timeless future together. But will it be in time?

PROLOGUE

As silence descended on the house, the shadows grew—dark grays and blacks that bled into each other. First one figure then another broke away, making a run toward the house. Silent as the grave, they moved swiftly over dew-slicked grass. Then they stopped still. Waiting. Not a movement betrayed them until a signal propelled them back into action

191

and they started crawling upwards. The walls damp coating no barrier to the intruders that ascended in the darkness.

The sound of each window breaking shattered the quiet—the figures were inside. Screams echoed through the night. Yet, in this area of large estates, heavy with noise-absorbing shrubbery, no one could hear those within. The blood-curdling screams went on and on before finally dying away.

Just one sound echoed through the night: The sobbing of a child.

The front door opened and figures trooped out—ghostly spectres against an inky night sky, broken by a single outline. A child in white, carried at the centre of the pack.

No sound broke the silence as they moved toward the trees surrounded the house.

Flames now licked at the manor: A deathly glow of oily smoke rising.

All that remained was a single person—wrapped in a cape of midnight blue beyond the house—watching them melt away.

Jemima moved toward the burning structure, breaking into a run as she breached the threshold. Vainly she attempted to enter, but the heat drove her back.

Now dashing tears from her face, she raced across the graveled driveway toward the gates, where the guardhouse was located. No sign of life existed within the building and some instinct of survival slowed her pace to a careful creep. Out of breath and heaving from exertion, she nervously checked within.

Small puffs of white vapor coloured the glass. She darted from one window to another. Her cloak drawn tightly around her body, hoping it would camouflage her from sight.

Satisfied, Jemima entered through the heavy, wooden front door and moved toward the phone she spied on the floor. Her eyes darting here and there she dialed, listening to the rotary motor as it returned to the proper position. Time was short and if *they* came back, she needed to have shared the message.

The phone rang once. Twice. With a brrping sound it connected.

"Hello?" A male answered and she felt a warm flush of relief at the voice. A voice she knew well.

"The manor has been breached. The girl child taken." The words erupted and her hand trembled.

"On our way." The click of the receiver being replaced echoed loudly in the stillness of the room.

Copper. She smelled copper.

Her stomach soured, knowing it meant more deaths. Jemima looked around for the gun—a gun with deadly, holy water-infused copper bullets—she knew was hidden somewhere in the room. A gun she couldn't find. *No divine intervention exists here*, she thought.

Hopefully *they* didn't remain. Feeding. If they were still here, that's what they would be doing. She found a corner and scrunched down, hiding from sight.

Crouched low, she tried to stay as still as possible, listening for sounds of the vehicles she knew would be coming. She dug her fingers into the flesh of her arms; remaining aware enough to stop before drawing blood. That would surely bring them out. Jemima dragged the cloak around her to capture the warmth, yet there was little to be found.

The sounds of engines roused her from the corner of the room. Jemima inched toward the window, the lead of the old glass distorting her view, hearing raised voices she knew Mistress Cressida had arrived.

Jemima retreated. Remained hidden from the woman because if she knew, all may well be lost. From the shadowed room she listened to the conversation...

"It smells like Estersham." The Mistress' eyes closed. "If it is, we have a problem." She turned once more, her face set and eyes now glacial in intensity. "James?"

The man nodded as if he knew what was to come.

"If I take those steps, I cannot return. Another must stand in my place." Her voice hardened while her eyes glittered in the dim light, piercing in their intensity.

Then the Mistress' voice called out in the near silence. "You and yours have been my loyal servants for so many years. I took an oath to protect you long ago. I renewed it with marriage and births, over and over. Now, my home and yours have been breached and this child taken from us. The girl child, who will be the hope and salvation of our kind, was ripped from the bosom of our nest. I will repay your loyalty and I will get her back." The words of power rippled in the night and licked at Jemima's skin.

Available in Ebook
books2read.com/BloodBride-Nix

Direct Autographed Copy
https://www.imogenenix.net/BloodBride

All That Glitters - a House Secrets Novella

Danu's Secrets

- The Downfall of Padraic O'Shaunessy
- A Demon Called Grace

The Automaton Series

- Haven House
- Nobel Crest
- Casa Bonita (Coming in 2024)

The Search Duology

- Miss Elspeth's Desire
- Miss Isabelle's Craving

Duology World Novels

- A Very Merry Widow

Reunion Trilogy

- War's End
- The Assassin
- Executing Justice

The Reunion Trilogy in Paperback

Sex Love & Aliens

- Tangled Webs
- False Webs
- Covert Webs

21st Testing Protocol

- Cyborg: Redux
- Children Of A Greater Evil
- When Evil Came To Stay
- Finis: The War To End All Wars

<u>Celtic Cupid Trilogy</u>

- Blame The Wine
- A Stranger's Embrace
- Revenge On Cupid

The Celtic Cupid Trilogy in Paperback

<u>Zombieology</u>

- The Reset
- I Dream of Zombies
- The Six Million Dollar Zombie
- Make Room For Zombies
- Days of Our Zombies
- Unnamed Zobiology title (coming soon)

<u>Knights of Pleasure</u>

- Silken Knights

<u>Single Titles</u>

The Chocolate Affair (also in Print)

Falling In Love Again (Previously A Sapphire For Karina)

BioCybe (also in Print)

Hesparia's Tears (also in Print)

Tomorrow's Promise

A Bar In Paris (also in Print)

Inheritance Of The Blood (also in Print)

The Plan

Loving Memories (also in Print)

Hero of Heartbreak Hill (also in Print)

My One & Only

Curse Bound

Non Fiction

Self Publishing: Absolute Beginners Guide (With Suzi Love)

Written as Ciara Cave

25 Curated Ways To Get Rid Of Telemarketers

Book Signings for Absolute Beginners

Imogene is published in a range of romance genres including Paranormal, Science Fiction and Contemporary. She is mainly published in the UK and USA.

In 2010, Imogene Nix (the pen name not Imogene herself) was born. Imogene sat down and worked tirelessly for 3 months culminating in the book Starline, which became the first in a trilogy titled, "Warriors of the Elector." Since then she's had over 30 titles published and is now focusing on hybridising herself - with a mixture of traditionally published and self-published works.

In fact, she's taking control of many of her back catalogue books, which are slowly re-releasing as self-published titles.

Imogene is a member of a range of professional organisations world wide, and believes in the mantra of mentoring and paying it forward and is actively involved in mentorship (through NaNoWrimo and her vlog: In The Chair With Imogene Nix) and tutoring of new and upcoming authors.

In her spare time she loves to drink coffee, wine & eat chocolate and is parenting her spoiled dog and a ferocious cat along with her family and looks forward to weekends away with her husband in their caravan "The Seven Year Hitch!" Do look forward to her caravan romance at some point!

To Contact Imogene
www.imogenenix.net
imogene@imogenenix.net